DEATH IN THE DESERT

Edge crept forward after hitching the reins of the horse to a clump of mesquite. The sun beat down on his back, sweat oozed from every pore in his body and he was breathing heavily from the climb. He paused only to survey the terrain in every direction. Nothing seemed to be moving out there, but Edge knew better than to trust the stillness.

And sure enough, it didn't take long for him to spot one of the sentries up ahead. The man failed to see the half-breed as he eased around a rock outcrop on the canyon rim. The eyes of the sentry were wide and staring. As Edge moved closer he realized the eyes were part of a savage death mask.

The boy in the ragged clothing sat with his back propped against a boulder, one of his limp hands still loosely fisted around the ancient Navy Colt in his lap. His dark hair was matted with congealed blood, but an area of stark white bone showed on the crown of his head where his skull had been shattered.

It was instinct, clear and sure, that suddenly informed Edge that he was not alone. How many more corpses would he have to discover before the sun set on this gruesome day? . . .

THE EDGE SERIES:

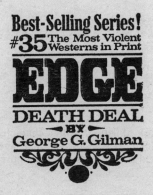

Best-Selling Series!
#35 The Most Violent Westerns in Print

EDGE

DEATH DEAL

BY

George G. Gilman

PINNACLE BOOKS   LOS ANGELES

EDGE #35: DEATH DEAL

Copyright © 1980 by George Gilman

A Pinnacle Books edition, published by special arrangement with New English Library, Ltd.

First printing, December 1980

ISBN: 0-523-40866-8

Cover illustration by Bruce Minney

Printed in the United States of America

PINNACLE BOOKS, INC.
2029 Century Park East
Los Angeles, California 90067

For D.M. who with a name like
his must know the code.

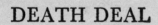

DEATH DEAL

CHAPTER ONE

THE stand of thirty-foot high pinyon pine trees provided welcome shade from the glare of the early afternoon Arizona Territory sun, and the man called Edge relished this more than the chunk of jerked beef he chewed on as he sat on the sandy ground, his back leaning against the reddish bark of one of the crooked trunks.

Likewise, his gray gelding appreciated the rest after a long morning's ride, but cropped without enthusiasm at a patch of arid scrub grass a few feet from where the man sat.

The man was some six foot three inches tall, solidly built with his close to two hundred pounds evenly distributed over a lean frame. Perhaps his face was handsome, or maybe it was ugly—opinions varied. It was made up of features drawn from a Mexican father and a northern European mother. The skin was dark from heritage and long exposure to the elements, deeply lined by the passing of almost forty years and by the harshness of his life during much of this time. The forehead was broad, the eyes ice-blue and permanently narrowed beneath hooded lids. The nose was hawklike, and below a Mexican-style moustache the mouth was thin and long. He had shaved at dawn but already the bristles sprouted thickly on his lean cheeks and along his firm jaw. Here and there among the stubble were traces of gray, although his hair, which he wore long enough to brush his shoulders, was still jet black.

He was dressed in a gray Stetson, low-crowned and

1

wide-brimmed, a shirt and kerchief of the same color, and black pants and spurless riding boots. There was an old leather gunbelt around his waist holding a Frontier Colt in the holster that was tied down to his right thigh. Encircling his throat, just visible above the sweat-stained kerchief, was a necklet of wooden beads which was not worn as an ornament. For the leather thong on which the beads were strung held, at the nape of his neck, a pouch into which was slotted a straight razor.

The man called Edge did not use this razor solely for shaving.

After he had chewed and swallowed the last of the dried beef, he rose from the base of the tree and moved across to the gelding. Where he unhooked one of the two canteens from the horn of the Western saddle and drank a little of the warm water. Then, as he re-capped the canteen and fixed it back on the saddle, he cocked his head, listening. At the same time the gelding stopped feeding and pricked his ears.

Hoofbeats sounded in the distance: several horses moving at a measured, unhurried pace. Then, a few moments later, other sounds revealed that the horses were a team hauling a rig of some sort. Coming down the north trail which intersected with the east-to-west trail beside which the pinyon stand grew.

Edge unhitched the gelding's reins from a saltbush and swung up into the saddle. But made no move to heel the horse out of the timber which concealed him from the trails.

"¡Buenos tardes!" a man shouted.

"Friggin' hell!" another roared.

A whip cracked in the hot air. And the cadence of hoofbeats and rolling wheels increased.

A fusillade of rifle-shots exploded and, against the diminishing echoes of the reports among the rock faces surrounding the intersection of the trails, the team-horses were given a counterorder to the gallop. And snorted as they brought the rig to a skidding halt.

"Is good!" the Mexican yelled in English above the

2

final sounds of the frenetic stop. "Everybody do like they are told and nobody get hurt! You understand this what I tell you?"

Edge, his lean features as impassive as when he was eating and drinking, had heeled his mount forward when the gunshots cracked. And was in a position to look down upon the scene at the trail intersection when the Concord of the Wells Fargo stage-line came to a rocking, dust-raising stop.

For the timber was clumped some two hundred feet up a gentle slope to the south of the east-west trail, directly opposite the gully from which the north trail emerged. At the mouth of the gully the soft sandstone cliff faces had crumbled to scatter boulders—some as large as two-storey houses—across the sandy ground on all sides of the meeting of the trails. And it was from the cover of some of these larger rocks that the six men wearing sombreros, dark-hued shirts and pants and kerchief-masks had stepped. To trigger warning shots from their Winchesters which were now aimed at the stalled stagecoach.

With the sun glaring harshly down from behind and to the west of the timber, the unmoving half-breed was as one with the deep shade cast by the pinyon pine. He reflected briefly as he watched the Mexicans close in on the stage from the front and either side, that they must have been in their ambush positions when he rode into the timber from the south.

"We ain't carryin' nothin' of value," the stage driver complained as his gloved hands opened and closed on the reins.

"You insult the *Señorita* Grace Worthington, *cuz!*" the obvious leader of the Mexicans snarled.

And shot the middle-aged, overweight driver. It was an apparently casual shot, triggered from the hip. But the bullet drilled through the man's heart and exploded out of his back in a welter of crimson droplets. The driver's grimace altered to an expression of surprise as he dropped the reins and half rose on the running-

3

board. Then his bulky frame twisted and he pitched headfirst off the side of the stage.

A woman screamed as dust motes rose from around the corpse and settled on it.

The expended shellcase from the Winchester glinted in the sunlight as it spun through the hot air after the Mexican had pumped the action of the rifle. Then he fired a third shot, in unison with those exploded by the other five masked men. All of them responding to the suicidal move of the suddenly terrified guard. He was of an age with the driver, but taller and thinner. But nobody missed the narrower target of his chest when he made to snatch up a rifle from the seat at his side and leap to the ground. He had the hammer cocked and was in mid-air when the six bullets ripped through his body. His mouth remained wide open, without having uttered a sound of terror, when he died and became limp. Then he hit the ground and was still. The blood that oozed from the entry and exit wounds was absorbed thirstily by the arid ground on which he lay.

The woman's scream was curtailed by a choked sob.

"Are you going to kill all of us?" a man called shakily from inside the Concord.

"What you do about it if I tell you yes?" the leader of the Mexicans answered. And vented a harsh laugh. "You pray, perhaps? Then you pray to me, *gringo*. Pray to Satanas! For it is I who have your life in my hands! Get out! All of you!"

He and one of his men had approached the stage from the front. Now he moved to join the two on the right of the Concord while the other man broke into a run along the west trail.

"The other door!" one of the men who had closed in on the left of the coach barked in Spanish.

And if his language was not understood, a menacing gesture with the rifle made the point. For the door on the right side of the Concord swung open and a short, fat man in his early sixties stepped nervously out into

4

the sunlight. His hands shook with fear as he reached up to assist a trembling woman from the coach. She was in the same age-group and was a match for his height. But very thin. Had the man not supported her when she was outside, she would have fallen: seemed to come within a hair's-breadth of fainting before he turned her to wrench her fixed stare away from the bullet-shattered body of the guard.

"You're well named, Satanas," another woman said from inside the coach, then emerged into the sunlight, the frown on her face deepening as she shifted her gaze from the corpse to the line of three rifle-toting Mexicans.

She was a tall, statuesque redhead, her lush hair long enough to reach midway down her back. Her face was classically beautiful, her complexion flawless in the shade of her broad hat-brim. It was a very feminine hat with a lot of lacy trimming on it. While her well-developed body and long legs were attired in a man's check shirt and Levis. The kerchief around her throat was knotted at the side. She was in her late twenties.

Her appearance caused the impassive half-breed in the trees to halt in the act of rolling a cigarette. Then, as Satanas vented another of his harsh laughs, Edge ran the paper across the tip of his tongue, twisted the cigarette once more between fingers and thumbs, and hung it unlit from a corner of his mouth. Growled, "Careful, lady, there could be the Devil to pay."

"*¡Sí, señorita!* I name myself this and everything I do, I do well."

"Except keep your word," Grace Worthington countered dully as she glanced again at the dead guard.

This as hoofbeats sounded and the two men on the other side of the Concord went to help their partner with the seven horses he had brought from where they were concealed around a curve of the west trail.

Satanas shrugged. "One *gringo* insulted you by saying you were of no value. The other tried to shoot us."

5

His tone of voice was dull now and he had begun to massage an area above his right eye with the tips of his fingers.

"Amigo, the horses, they are here," the Mexican on his right said in Spanish.

"Take her," he answered in the same language. Then, to Grace Worthington, "You will come with us, señorita."

"Why?" She sounded defiant rather than afraid.

The man to Satanas' left countered, "Because if you do not, we will kill these old people. It will not be hard for us and you will come anyway."

"Oh, Miss Worthington," the frail elderly woman cried.

"Don't worry, Mrs. Benteen," the redhead said. "I don't think they intend to harm me."

She complied with the tacit command of two gesturing rifles and moved to where the group of seven horses had been halted. The men who waved the Winchesters went with her.

"You!" Satanas growled, glaring at the fat man.

"Yes?" As Mrs. Benteen clung to him.

"You are not a doctor, are you? I keep getting a bad pain in my head. If you are a doctor perhaps you can give me something."

A shake of the head. "I'm Cyrus Benteen. The lawyer in Indian Hill."

Satanas snorted. Then, "Lawyer, uh? Hey, I like that. Lawyers, they are supposed to be honorable men. This makes you perfect man to carry message to Mr. Kane Worthington of the Indian Hill Ranch, I think."

"Oh dear," Mrs. Benteen gasped.

"You tell Mr. Kane Worthington that Satanas has his firstborn daughter, uh. And you tell him not to worry about her. He will hear from me soon. And still he will not need to worry. For he will have no trouble getting the money I will need to bring his daughter back to him. You tell him, uh?"

Both Mr. and Mrs. Benteen, faces fixed with shock,

6

were shifting their eyes from Satanas to the now mounted Grace Worthington and back again. The leader of the Mexicans, still troubled by a nagging ache in his head, lost patience, and exploded a shot into the ground a few feet in front of the couple.

"You tell him, uh!" His voice was an angry bellow.

"Yes, yes, I'll tell Mr. Worthington," Benteen answered.

"Is good, *gringo*."

He swung away from them, strode to the horses and joined his men in the saddle. All of them booted their rifles. Then, with one of the men gripping the bridle of the horse carrying the captive woman, the whole bunch heeled their mounts into a gallop. Heading along the east trail, then veering to the side to ride up the slope beyond the timber in which Edge was concealed. Their dust settled and the sound of hoofbeats faded from earshot.

Edge struck a match on the stock of the booted Winchester and heeled his horse out of the timber. And such was the intensity of the silence after the Mexicans had gone that Mrs. Benteen heard the scrape of match head on rifle stock and snapped her eyes toward the pinyon stand, saw the half-breed the moment he emerged from the shade. She gasped, clung more tightly to her husband and infected him with her new fear.

The half-breed rode slowly down the slope as Benteen joined his wife in watching the approach. Like his hearing, the eyesight of the city-suited lawyer had decayed faster than that of the woman and he was obviously straining to see why she was so perturbed by the appearance of the stranger. And when Edge came into sharp focus, Benteen's own concern was negated. For the tall, lean man astride the gray gelding touched the brim of his hat and parted his thin lips to show white teeth in a smile of greeting.

"Mrs. Benteen. Mr. Benteen."

"You know Amelia and me, sir?"

A shake of the head as Edge reined his horse to a

halt, close enough to the elderly couple for them to see that there was not a degree of warmth in the narrowed eyes of the man. "Saw what happened here. Heard the names mentioned."

"You saw what happened? And made no attempt to intervene?" There was shock and anger in the woman's voice and quivering on her thin features.

Edge swung down from the saddle. "You tired of living, ma'am?"

"I beg your pardon?"

"The gentleman means we are still alive, my dear," Cyrus Benteen said. "There were six of them and if he had moved against them there would undoubtedly have been further bloodshed."

His wife was unimpressed and expressed tacit contempt as Edge checked the stage team and the wheels of the Concord.

"Indian Hill far from here?"

"Five miles." Benteen pointed the short finger of a pudgy hand along the west trail.

"Can you handle the stage?"

"Aren't you going to help us, young man?" the woman blurted.

"Figure there's someone else needs help more than you, ma'am."

"Of course. Grace." She was shamefaced.

"Her, too," Edge allowed as he grabbed the body of the guard under the armpits and backed up the step and into the stage, dragging the burden aboard. Then he got out the other side and loaded the corpse of the driver in a similar manner.

"Who else?" Mrs. Benteen asked as Edge got off the stage, closed the door and flicked away his half-smoked cigarette.

"Me, ma'am."

The woman snorted her disgust. While her husband grunted and scowled.

"If you think you can make capital out of this trouble, sir, you are doubtless correct," the lawyer growled.

8

"Kane Worthington is a wealthy man who will pay highly for the safe return of his daughter."

With the corpses riding inside the Concord, the woman elected to climb up onto the box-seat.

"My ma used to tell me the Lord helps those who help themselves," the half-breed said as he swung astride the gelding and Cyrus Benteen sat on the driver's seat beside his wife. "Does Grace have a mother still?"

"Gertrude died some ten years ago," Amelia Benteen replied tautly while her husband cautiously released the brake lever and nervously took up the reins.

"Explains it, maybe."

"Explains what?"

"No Mrs. Worthington to tell her daughter not to go on the stage."

CHAPTER TWO

TRACKING Satanas, his men and their kidnap victim was easy over the first five miles. For the Mexicans had no reason to assume they were being followed as they rode at a casual pace out of the Quijotoa Valley of Arizona Territory toward the border with Sonora, Mexico. And perhaps they were confident, too, that the message to be delivered by Cyrus Benteen to Kane Worthington would ensure no search would be mounted later.

Certainly the kidnappers made no attempt to cover their backtracks for those first few minutes. And Edge needed merely to glance at the soft, hoofprinted ground every now and then to check that he was still on the trail of his quarry.

So, for most of the time, he was able to maintain a careful watch on the rugged terrain which spread out on all sides of him. He rode easy in the saddle, his casual attitude offering no clue to the degree of caution with which his slitted eyes made their survey from out of the deep shade of his hat-brim. Or that, just beneath the surface of his relaxed posture, he was keyed up and ready to respond instantly to the first sign that danger threatened.

And the threat of danger was always with this man called Edge. It had been so for many years—had started when his name was Josiah C. Hedges and he rode away from the Iowa farm where he was born and raised, to enlist in the Union army and fight in the War Between the States.

During that long and brutal war, tens of thousands of

men had endured the rigors of constant danger. This man more than most, perhaps, because of circumstances which as a lieutenant of cavalry and then a captain caused him to be in command of six men who were often as eager to kill him as the enemy. Then the war came to an end and Hedges rode back to the farm, anxious to forget the awful lessons in the art of killing he had been forced to learn, and to enjoy the rewards of peace with his young and crippled brother.

But the farm had been burned and Jamie was dead—brutally tortured and murdered by the six men who had survived the war because of their captain's leadership. Every fiber of Hedges' body demanded vengeance and he took it—using the war-taught skills to track down and punish the murderers of his kid brother. And it was during this bitter process that he changed his name to Edge. Much else was changed, too. The man himself and his aims. Not by design. Instead, by the hand of his cruel, ruling fate.

And he became a loner and a drifter, doomed to ride countless trails across dangerous ground, each new experience with violence hardening him both physically and emotionally and driving deeper into him the certain knowledge that there could be no other way of life for him.

For a long time he had sought to defy such a destiny. To establish something—somewhere and somehow—close to the peaceful and prosperous life which the farm in Iowa had promised. But always such hopes were violently dashed and he was left with only grief and survival as his rewards. And thus he learned the hardest lesson of all. That it was necessary for him to admit defeat, to offer unconditional surrender to his ruling fate. To give up hope for anything other than continued survival. To form no deep relationship with anybody. To meet trouble head on, deal with it and ride away. To earn money wherever and whenever he could. To kill or be killed with total lack of concern for the innocent victims of the violence, with the full knowledge that none of them cared about him.

And abiding by just one rule—that he dealt fairly with those who were fair to him and took no more than he considered he was owed from those who sought to cheat him.

Which was why he had shot the horse of a man named Adam Steele.*

His thin lips drew back from his teeth as he recalled the incident in the town of Southfields. And of the violent events which preceded it. Pleased that he had not killed the Virginian dude before setting off on the new trail which had led him here. For Steele and he, so dissimilar in many ways, shared a great deal of common ground. Dangerous ground. And the half-breed found it strangely comforting to be aware that he was not unique, that there was at least one other man riding the western states and territories in the same emotional void as he.

No other man of any kind showed himself against the sun-parched, almost lifeless terrain across which Edge traveled on the trail of the Mexicans and their prisoners. But, as he neared the border, he did not consider his careful surveillance a futile waste of effort. And when the trail became more difficult to follow he did not abandon his watchfulness in every direction to concentrate entirely on the harder-to-find sign.

It was a change of terrain rather than any decision by the Mexicans which meant Edge had to take more care in his pursuit. For the ground became rocky as it sloped upwards toward the Sierra Madres of Sonora, with just scattered and infrequent pockets of sandy soil in which cactus plants, mesquite and greasewood clumps maintained a tenuous grip on existence. Here and there a hoofprint showed, but for the most part the tangible signs of the group's progress took the form of horse-droppings, used matches and cheroot stubs. But when

* Edge and Steele: Two of a Kind.

13

these were not in evidence, the half-breed worked on the logical assumption that, insurmountable obstacles apart, Satanas was taking his prisoner in the same direction as at the start: due south.

In the late afternoon Edge was able to increase his pace from the walk to which he had held the gelding until now. For he saw signs which led into a deep canyon: broad at the mouth but quickly narrowing until its hundred-foot-high walls came to within two hundred feet of each other. There could be no deviation from the canyon and with deep shade thrown by the western rock face, it was cool enough on the smooth floor for the gelding to be cantered for short lengths of time.

He covered perhaps two miles with alternate canters and walks. Then dismounted and led the horse by the reins along snake-like twists in the canyon where it was at its narrowest. Beyond this area, the walls drew apart again and lost height and steepness on a broad, rock-littered and crater-pocked slope. At the crest of the rise the skyline was jagged, featured with rocky high points and clumps of wind-bent desert brush, where far more than a half-dozen riflemen could stand secret guard and command an unobstructed view of anyone moving out of the canyon and up the grade.

The sun was low by then, but still at least an hour away from setting behind a distant ridge. So Edge rested for the time it took, unsaddling his horse and hobbling him in a pocket of cover a few yards in from the canyon's end. Animal and man drank sparingly, but neither ate.

As he sat with his hat tipped forward over his stubbled face, back leaning against the canyon wall, Edge felt no sense of wasting the time that was slipping away as afternoon retreated from evening. Perhaps the camp of Satanas and his men was many miles from here. And even if it were just beyond the jagged ridge of the hill, maybe no guards had been posted to watch the canyon. But man and mount needed to rest after a long day's ride, so time spent thus was not wasted.

He chose twilight to check on the ridge, leaving his horse hobbled but taking his Winchester from the boot. And used the shadowed cover of the west wall until it ran out halfway up the six-hundred-foot-long slope. Then zigzagged between rocks and hollows to attain his objective. The gloom of twilight in such country as this was short-lived and he was only three-quarters of the way to the top when the near full moon spread glittering, blue light across the high desert terrain. But no one challenged him as he cast a long, moving shadow among the unmoving areas of blackness on the white rocky surface.

Then his shadow became as one with many overlapping patches of darkness at the top of the slope. And he dropped onto his haunches, drew in a deep breath and smelled smoke. He breathed out and sucked in more air, this time through his nose. Mixed in with the woodsmoke was an appetizing aroma of cooking food.

He started forward again, moving in a half-crouch, around rocks and between patches of vegetation, toward a thin column of gray smoke that rose straight as a flagstaff in the rapidly cooling air. And the closer he got to the source of the smoke, the more sounds were picked up by his straining ears.

Fifty feet from where he had entered the cover, he went down onto his belly and inched forward: came to a halt at the top of a sheer drop. And looked down upon the camp of Satanas, his lean features arranged in their habitual impassive set as he saw that Grace Worthington was a long way from being an unwilling prisoner of the Mexicans.

The red-headed woman was seated in a padded armchair on the stoop of a single-storey adobe building. And spilled some liquid from a glass clutched in her hand as she threw back her head and laughed at something Satanas had said. The Mexican bandit chief was sprawled in a matching chair on the other side of a low table from the woman. And topped up her glass, then refilled his own, from a bottle on the table. A heap of

15

salt in a bowl beside the bottle indicated it was tequila they were drinking.

There had once been a half-dozen buildings on the floor of the east-to-west canyon into which Edge looked down. But all that remained of the others were the foundations. While here and there were signs that a wall had at one time enclosed the buildings, so this had probably been a *Federale* post in the past.

Now it was the stronghold of Satanas and his twenty or so bandits—along with half as many women—who would have ample room to bed down in the long, low building on the stoop of which the chief and the American woman were sharing a bottle and a joke. While the Mexican women prepared a meal on the recently lit fire at the center of the former compound and carried trestle tables and chairs from out of the building.

A half-dozen men sat on the ground or their saddles, drinking and smoking. But Edge estimated the strength of Satanas' band from the twenty horses enclosed in a rope corral out back of the building.

The canyon was perhaps forty feet deep and two hundred feet wide at this point. To the east it appeared to come to a dead end, while to the west it ran for about a half-mile before it curved southwards. The camp where preparations were being made for a feast was sited at a midway point between the canyon walls, well lit by the fire and the moon.

Taking care to ensure that a clump of brush prevented him from being skylined, Edge thrust himself forward to peer over the rim of the canyon wall. And saw that a narrow pathway angled steeply down its otherwise sheer face—wide enough for a man to lead a horse. Or ride if he trusted the surefootedness of his mount. The top of the pathway was twenty feet to the right of where the half-breed drew back into solid cover. But continued to watch and listen to the scene below him.

The good-humored mood of Satanas and the American woman seemed to be shared by everyone else in the

16

camp and even those engaged in the chores of preparing the meal were in high spirits. The women laughing and giggling and submitting willingly to the intimate caresses of some of the men whenever they strayed within reach of eager hands.

The sounds of merriment reached up to Edge as a discordant body of noise, with just the occasional shrieked word ringing out clearly. In Spanish. Mixed in with exclamations which had no single nationality.

"Vaya a . . . "

"Ooch!"

" *. . . comida . . .* "

" *. . . vaca . . .* "

"Aaaaah . . ."

"Esto me gusta."

Once, from Satanas, " *. . . dinero."*

Followed by shrill laughter from Grace Worthington—intermingled with words, one of which was ". . . father . . . "

Then, some ten minutes after the half-breed had reached his vantage-point, the rest of the men emerged from the building—stretching their arms and legs and yawning as if just roused from sleep. There was a period of good-natured trading of insults while, on the stoop, Satanas seemed to be naming many of his men for the eager-to-learn Grace Worthington. For their part, the newly awakened bandits paid scant attention to the American woman and, like every other man except for the chief, seemed interested only on the forthcoming meal.

But the huge cuts of beef were not yet spit-roasted and the chili beans had only just been poured in the cooking pot. So more bottles of tequila were brought from the building, along with two guitars. And while the food was cooking the darkly clad bandits and their women garbed in shapeless white dresses filled the time with drinking, singing and dancing.

Santanas watched all this with the air of a benevolent family patriarch, occasionally pouring fresh drinks for

17

himself and Grace Worthington and every now and then replying to a question she posed.

Edge continued to hear the sounds of the alfresco party but he now only glanced from time to time at the happy Mexicans and their American "prisoner." This as he crawled on hands and knees down the steep and narrow pathway which canted across the canyon's north wall—keeping low to avoid being seen in dark silhouette against the moon-lighted rock face.

He moved slowly for two reasons. It was an additional safeguard against his being spotted. And passing time was an ally—the more the bandits had to drink, the better his chances of success.

As he reached the canyon floor and bellied into the cover of a clump of mesquite, the drinking was interrupted and the music was curtailed.

"We eat now, my friends!" Satanas yelled after stamping a foot on the stoop-boarding to get the attention of the revellers. "The food will be good! The wine, too! But it will be as fodder for the burro of the poorest peon in all Mexico compared with the feast we will enjoy after the outcome of today's events!"

He made the announcement in his native language and as he escorted Grace Worthington toward the head of the trestle-table he seemed to be giving her a translation in English—while his men and their women cheered a gleeful response to his speech.

Then the eating began, the Mexicans attacking the food like ravenous animals, washing down each mouthful with wine which they drank from the bottle. Only now did the beautiful red-headed woman reveal a sign of being disconcerted in this company; wore an expression of disdain for a few moments as she watched the Mexicans scoop up meat and beans in their fingers and thrust the food into their mouths. Then pass wine bottles one to the other, with the neck still sticky from the contents of the last mouth to suck from it. She even wrinkled her nose and started to form her lips into the line of a sneer when she saw that Satanas had abandoned his former good-mannered attitude and was behaving as crudely as the rest.

Edge heard the unmistakable click of a gun hammer being thumbed back. At the same moment as the muzzle was pressed into the small of his back.

"What you think, *gringo*," a man said quietly. "The *señorita* who is our guest seems no longer to be enjoying the party, uh?"

The half-breed subdued the rising self-anger that he had allowed the man to get the drop on him so easily. Continued to direct his narrow-eyed gaze at Grace Worthington as she submitted to the laughing encouragement of the bandit chief and entered into the debauched spirit of the feast.

"Tell you, feller," he muttered with a sigh. "For a while there she sure looked like she was going to throw up from the rotten smell of excess."

CHAPTER THREE

"YOU will release the rifle, raise your hands above your head and stand up, *gringo*. If you do not do these things, I will kill you."

Edge believed the soft-spoken, young-sounding Mexican and he complied with the orders, rising from behind the mesquite, his hands up, level with his shoulders.

"You've been there a long time, I figure?"

There was a low sound of splashing water behind the half-breed and he realized the man was urinating. The light pressure of the gun muzzle against his back had not altered from the time he first felt it.

"I watch you from canyon rim to here. From the cave where I live. But I could wait no longer to see what you planned."

"There are times when a man's got to do what a man's got to do, feller. Only natural."

"We go to Satanas now," the Mexican ordered, as he finished emptying his bladder and smoothly transferred his hand to the butt of the half-breed's Colt, slid the revolver from the holster.

Without aggression, Edge glanced to the side as he stepped around the mesquite. And saw one of the areas of dark shadow at the base of the canyon wall was not just another shallow cleft in the rock, was deep enough to be termed a cave. The ground between its mouth and the clump of mesquite was soft sand.

The gun muzzle was no longer tight to his back and he heard the clink of metal on metal as his captor stooped to pick up the Winchester with the same hand that held the confiscated Colt.

"Keep walking, *gringo*. To kill you will be no hardship."

"Matter of opinion, feller," Edge growled wryly.

This as the sounds of merriment at the long table faltered and died with the turning of heads toward the approaching prisoner and his gun-toting escort. The smiles on the faces of the Mexicans were displaced by scowls, frowns, grimaces and expressions of perplexed curiosity. Only Grace Worthington showed dumbstruck fear as she stared at the unexpected intruder.

"What is this we have here?" Satanas demanded to end the silence which the half-breed's sudden appearance had heralded.

"I capture him for you, Satanas!" the man in back of Edge supplied, sounding younger than ever as his voice grew shrill with excitement. "I see him watching the feast and I capture him! I do this myself!"

Hands which had moved to drape the butts of holstered revolvers were withdrawn. And smiles returned to many faces. And shouts of *"Bravo"* and *"Bueno, Nino!"* rang out the half-breed's rifle and revolver were tossed onto the table.

Still in the grip of fear, Grace Worthington tugged at the shirt sleeve of Satanas and pleaded to be told what Nino had reported.

"The kid's very proud of putting the arm on me all by himself, lady," Edge said, as he halted close to the head of the table, across from where she sat on the right of the chief.

"You understand the language, uh?" Satanas growled into another brief silence which had followed the half-breed's terse explanation. And he stared hard into the lean, dark-skinned face. Nodded. *"Si,* I think you are not all *gringo,* uh?"

Another nod, accompanied by a grin. "That will be no trouble. We are close to the border here. So we can bury you so that you rest half in Mexico and half in the United States, uh?"

He vented a harsh laugh and many of his men echoed the sound.

Satanas was about forty and was a handsome man, with a solidly built frame a fraction under six feet tall. Like most of his men, who were in the thirty-to-forty age-group, he wore a Mexican-style moustache which was clearly defined despite the day-long stubble which sprouted on every face. There was a glint of innate cunning in the bandit chief's small and dark eyes. But, Edge was prepared to admit, under different circumstances he would probably have termed it intelligence.

"Which part of you you want where, uh?"

" 'It's my funeral, but I guess I'll leave the arrangements up to you, feller."

Satanas laughed again.

"Let me kill him, please," Nino asked in Spanish. "I can do it, I know I can!"

Edge shifted his bleak-eyed gaze to Nino, who was a short, skinny boy of sixteen or so with hollow cheeks and a wide, slack mouth. His skin was blotched by acne. He was barefoot and dressed in ragged white pants and shirt. His right hand was fisted around the butt of an old Navy Colt with the front sight bent and the tip of the hammer broken off.

"The killing is easy, boy," the half-breed told the eager youngster in his native language. "It's the living that can be hard. Afterwards. With yourself."

Satanas thudded the table with his fist. And the sudden anger which showed in his scowl was heard in his voice. "We speak English! For the sake of our beautiful guest."

He raised the fist, opened it and massaged his forehead with the food-sticky fingertips.

"I guess you know nothing of doctoring, uh *gringo*?"

"What do you know, mister?" Grace Worthington demanded huskily, still staring fixedly up at Edge's impassive face. "What are you doing here?"

23

"Standing with egg on my face, lady," he drawled. "And that ain't the kind that eases an empty belly."

Satanas used a Bowie knife to spear a chunk of chili drenched beef and thrust it toward the half-breed. "Eat hearty, *gringo*. That's what a condemned man is supposed to do."

The Mexican women, all in their early twenties and pretty, laughed with as much gusto as the men. While Edge took the meat and bit into it.

"Answer me, Mr. . . . whatever your name is!" the American woman demanded, her voice still husky.

"Edge, Miss Worthington."

"You know my name!" She snapped her head around to stare at Satanas. "He knows my name!"

The bandit chief shrugged. "So he knows your name. How long was he watching and listening to us, Nino?"

"An hour at least, *amo*. But perhaps he was up on the rim much longer. A man who knows too much, he should die."

"I said a guard should have been posted," a scar-faced man with a broken nose growled from beside Grace Worthington.

"In English!" Satanas snarled at the man who Edge recognized as one of those who had been at the stage hold-up. "You are so smart, Jose, you think you are ready to take over from me already?"

Jose flinched from the power of the chief's anger. Muttered sulkily, *"Dispenseme, amo."* Then, quickly, "Excuse me, boss."

"How do we know he is alone?" the American woman posed, her frightened eyes raking their gaze along the rim of the canyon's north wall.

"I'm alone," Edge said evenly after swallowing a final piece of the good-tasting meat.

"But you will die among good company, *gringo,*" Nino growled.

"You've got a one-track mind, kid," the half-breed told him.

"And you have a nerve of iron, *Señor* Edge," Satanas countered levelly, no longer good-humored after the display of anger toward Jose. Instead, seemed intrigued by the half-breed. "Why are you not afraid of us?"

"If you scared me, feller, I wouldn't have trailed you from where you held up the stage."

Grace Worthington gasped.

"We did not see you." Satanas was suspicious now.

"You weren't meant to."

Fresh anger glinted in the cunning eyes. "I see you now, Edge," he said tautly. "Why are you not afraid that I will have you killed—perhaps as additional entertainment for our celebration feast?"

"Corpses carry no messages, feller."

Anger gave way to interest. "Messages, *gringo*?"

"Figure you're celebrating a little early." He was confident enough about the curiosity he had aroused in Satanas to reach out and pick up another hunk of beef. "You've got the goods to sell but you haven't made contact with the buyer yet."

"I am not goods for sale, you cold-hearted sonofabitch!" Grace Worthington flung at him.

Then screamed as Satanas swung an arm and struck her a heavy, back-handed blow to the cheek. He hit her so hard that her chair rocked and she would have toppled backwards out of it had Jose not grabbed her. Many of the Mexican women smiled their pleasure at the attack as the rich man's daughter was gripped by a new kind of shock and fear.

"You are supposed to be a *damisela*—a fine lady!" the bandit chief snarled, merely glancing at the distressed woman. Then moderated his tone to add, "You would not use such language at your home. Do not use it at mine. *Señor* Edge, why should I trust you to be my messenger, uh?"

The half-breed began to roll a cigarette as he chewed a final mouthful of meat. "Because I'm available, feller."

Satanas waved a hand to encompass the company

aligned along each side of the table. "So are many others. And I know well and trust every man and woman here."

"I will be honored to do your bidding, *amo*," Nino offered enthusiastically.

Satanas grinned broadly. "You see, *gringo*? Even this boy who crept into our camp unbidden many weeks ago and who has been treated worse than a scavenging dog from that day to this—he is eager to serve me."

Edge nodded as he struck a match on the table and lit the cigarette. "Just trying to stay alive and make a dishonest dollar, feller."

"There are easier ways to do this than coming to the camp of Satanas, *gringo*. And I do not think that you came here, like Nino, to offer your services to me."

The half-breed shrugged. "Took an opportunity that was offered me."

"To try to take the *Señorita* Worthington from me."

Edge showed a wry smile. "There were just six of you at the hold-up."

"Kill him and let the *fiesta* continue, *amo*!" a man at the far end of the table called. "I am tired of this talk."

There were sounds of agreement. But Satanas was again troubled by a stabbing pain above his right eye. And he thudded the table with the heel of a fist and glared his men and their women into sullen silence.

"Indio! You are like Jose, uh? You wish to be the *amo*? You want to give the orders? You want to start right now, uh?"

"*Dispense usted*, Satanas," the tall, broad-shouldered and big-bellied part-Indian responded humbly.

The bandit chief nodded his satisfaction with the apology and the servile attitude of the rest of his group. Then, as he gently massaged his aching head, he shifted his cunning eyes back to the impassive face of Edge.

"You know why I did not have you killed right away, *gringo*?"

The half-breed smiled with his mouth. Still managing to conceal the ice-cold fear that was concentrated at the

26

pit of his stomach, knowing from experience that the irascible and ruthless Satanas was as capable of blasting a man to death as of slapping the face of a woman—if the impulse struck him. But for now the Mexican's wrath was directed at his own people and the humiliated Grace Worthington.

"It's only bad luck that I question, feller." He arced the partially smoked cigarette into the fire and grimaced. "And that not very often."

"I think you are a man of considerable courage. Most men . . ." He glowered at the sullen faces of his band. " . . . would have turned and run when they saw not just six *bandidos*. Would have abandoned such a dangerous mission. Or have gone for help. You chose to come closer. At great risk. Such a courageous man should not be shot down like a prowling coyote. So I give you the chance to bargain for your life, *Señor* Edge. If I am not interested in what you have to sell, then I will kill you. Personally. With honor."

The pain in his head receded and he leaned back in his chair, arms akimbo and with a receptive expression on his good-looking face. While Edge nodded his agreement to the deal and decided there was a slim chance of snatching the Navy Colt from the hand of the disappointed Nino and putting a bullet into Satanas before his own body was ripped apart by a fusillade of shots from the guns of the other men. It would be a bad way to die, but then, there was no good way.

"Benteen told me Kane Worthington's a rich man who'll pay high for having his daughter returned to him, feller," the half-breed said evenly. "Figured he'd pay higher if I brought her to him than if I just told him where you were keeping her. Greater the risk, better the reward."

"*Si.*" Satanas drank some wine from a bottle. "But you failed."

"I stop him," Nino said proudly.

"*¡Silencio, cuz!*" He glowered at the boy then nod-

27

ded to Edge. "But you have seen that the *Señorita* Worthington is a willing visitor to our camp."

"It's Kane Worthington's money that interests me, feller. Don't give a damn about his family problems."

Grace Worthington scowled.

"It is his money that interests all of us, *gringo*. Why should you have a share of what we intend to get?" Satanas showed an avaricious grin. "Fifty thousand dollars, it is a great amount. But the division, it has already been agreed."

"I'll add my commission on the top."

"For doing what?"

"Delivering your demand to Worthington, getting the money from him and bringing it to wherever you want."

"You say you saw the hold-up of the stage, *gringo*." Satanas answered coldly. "Then you saw me kill a man for insulting the *señorita*. I think now you insult me. My intelligence. When you have the money—fifty, a hundred, two hundred thousand dollars—how can I be sure you will not take it all for yourself? For you have no reason to be concerned for the fate of this lady."

Edge shook his head. "Better if I double-crossed you by bringing her pa and a bunch of guns here to get the woman back by force, feller. Figure he'd pay me well for that and I'd be able to live high off the hog without always looking over my shoulder."

"*Si, gringo.* You speak my thoughts. And it sounds like you are talking yourself to death."

"Or into a job. The Benteens saw that you and your men were Mexican." He shrugged. "Now I don't know what kind of a set-up there is at the Worthington spread. Or how hard it is to get to the big man. Or how much he knows about his daughter's feelings toward him."

The half-breed knew he could be talking himself up a blind alley but he continued along the same course because he was committed to practicing the theory that while there was talking there would be no killing. Knew, also, that there was not a single solid reason why

28

Satanas should not kill him. Unless the Mexican was close to being as ignorant of the Indian Hill Ranch set-up as was Edge himself.

"My father has no idea in the world that I am a willing kidnap victim!" Grace Worthington blurted. "He dotes on both May and myself. Kill him, Felipe! He will ruin every—"

The man at the head of the table banged down his fist again. Directly in front of her, causing her plate to bounce. And the woman flinched away from him. "I do not allow my men to tell me what to do!" he roared. "You will hold your tongue, *damisela*! Or I will cut it out and send it to your rich father as evidence that I mean business!"

"But Felipe—"

"Satanas! My name is Satanas!"

A heavy silence followed his thunderous words. Edge broke it.

"I don't know what kind of a man Kane Worthington is, feller. Maybe he's sitting at home right now, sweating with worry about his daughter. If he is, you got no use for me. You or any of your men will be able to ride right up to the house and fix up the deal. But men who get as rich and powerful as I hear Kane Worthington is, they ain't usually the kind to sit still and hope in a situation like this."

"That *gringo* is one mean bastard," Satanas growled. And took a swallow of wine, smashed the bottle on the table and yelled, "*¡Necesito tequila!*" A bottle was brought to him by one of the women and he demanded of Edge, "Tell me what you have in mind, uh?"

"I look more American than Mexican, feller. And the Benteens can vouch that I took off on your trail after the hold-up. I figure I can get to Worthington without any trouble."

Satanas took a long drink of tequila and growled, "Then what?"

"I'll ask for the fifty thousand you want. Plus two

grand for myself. And I'll bring it to wherever you plan to make the exchange."

"La Hondonada." He waved the bottle toward the north. "The canyon beyond this one. But why should not Jose, or Indio, or Ricardo, or Esteban, or even Nino do this? For I do not believe that Worthington will refuse to see anybody who has news of his daughter. Mexican, American, or anybody. And he will pay to have his daughter returned to him. No matter if he hates her as much as she hates him. A man as powerful as he, it is a matter of principle."

His men grunted their agreement. Then all eyes raked to the face of Edge and it was obvious to the half-breed that all the Mexicans—and Grace Worthington—considered he had failed to talk himself out of this life-or-death corner. So he voiced the clincher that would decide his fate—and maybe, if he was fast enough—that of Satanas, too.

"Okay, feller. Seems you've thought this thing through pretty well. But there's always a weak point in any kidnapping of this kind. You have to get a message to the man with the money. And unless you use the mail or the telegraph, you have to send a messenger. You send one of your own men, you risk having him become just as much of a hostage as the woman."

Moon and firelight illuminated faces that abruptly showed concern. And worried eyes shifted away from the half-breed to gaze quizzically at Satanas. For a moment the man at the head of the table was disconcerted. Then his bristled features formed into a pensive frown.

"He's talking nonsense!" Grace Worthington exclaimed. "If there's a chance of getting me back unharmed, father wouldn't dare risk—"

"*Silencio,*" Satanas cut in, not harshly. And waved a hand to indicate that his command was directed at everyone. Then, after stretched seconds of thought, he asked of Edge, "I say again, why should I trust you when you have the money, *gringo*?"

"Kane Worthington will take care of that, feller.

When he gives me the money, he won't just wish me good luck and wave me goodbye."

The Mexican nodded, his face still furrowed by the thoughtful frown. Then, abruptly, he set the bottle down on the table and nodded. "You have a deal, *Señor* Edge."

"But—" Grace Worthington blurted. And the rest of what she had to say was swamped by a burst of loud-voiced Spanish protests. Then the din was abruptly curtailed by another scream of pain from the American woman and the sight of Satanas grasping a handful of her hair, jerking her head to the side and lashing out with a knife.

"Here," he said coldly, thrusting the severed locks toward the half-breed. "You will take this to Kane Worthington. And you will tell him that if he does not give you fifty thousand dollars to bring to La Hondo-nada at noon the day after tomorrow, I will send him the head from which it comes."

"*¡Satanas, ésto no me gusta!*" a man protested, leaping to his feet as Edge took the fistful of hair.

"Sit down, Ricardo," the bandit chief instructed in the same cold tone as before.

"*No, está loco—*"

Satanas sighed, as if in resignation. But under cover of this attitude he drew the Army Colt from his holster, cocked the hammer before the gun showed above the table and shot the small-of-stature Ricardo in the heart. A difficult shot over a range of ten feet as the man and woman flanking Ricardo scrambled to get clear and the victim himself made to twist away from the aimed revolver.

Perhaps Ricardo was still alive when he sat down in the chair. But he was dead a moment later, folding forward to sprawl across the table, knocking plates and bottles aside.

"Anybody else wish to question my decision, *com-padres*?" Satanas asked, as he cocked the Colt and then blew into the white muzzle smoke that drifted across his face.

Shocked eyes were shifted from the inert corpse to the bandit chief. There was a question on every lip, but it remained unspoken as fear took an icy grip on every man and woman seated at the table.

"Amo, yo—" Nino started.

"Silencio," Jose advised softly.

"I figure they all want to know why, feller," Edge said.

Some of the Mexicans glanced at him, resentfully afraid that the remark would stoke the fires of Satanas's cold anger. But then, as their chief eased forward the hammer and slid the Colt into his holster, tacit relief became as tangible as the previous fear had been.

"That is two questions, *gringo,*" the man at the head of the table answered evenly, and got to his feet. "Why did I kill Ricardo? I killed him because he disobeyed my order and questioned my authority as leader. It is not the first time I have had to take such action. But it is many months since such an example was set."

He bit the end of a cigar and allowed his dark eyes to rake across every face at the table before he struck a match and lit the tobacco. He nodded his satisfaction with the way that none of his men or their women were able to hold his unblinking gaze.

"The second question concerns why I have decided to make use of you, *gringo.* It is not necessary for a leader to explain his actions to his men. But this time, I make an exception, uh?" Now he grinned at the members of his band. "To show that while I am prepared to kill any one of them . . ." He clicked a finger and thumb. " . . . like that, I also have great respect for them."

He left his place at the head of the table and moved to where the half-breed's Colt and Winchester lay. He picked up both guns and handed them to Edge, holding them by the barrels. A few gasps accompanied the action.

"The *Señorita* Grace Worthington did co-operate in coming into our hands, *gringo,*" he went on, speaking the words harshly through teeth clenched to the cigar.

"The whole thing was my idea, Felipe—Satanas!" the American woman blurted.

"Jose?" The chief made a gesture with a clenched fist. And grunted, "Uh?"

The man with the broken nose and a scar on his right cheek merely had to half turn in his chair to send a short but powerful punch into the side of the woman's jaw. She was unconscious before she could utter another sound and she toppled from her chair and became an untidy heap on the floor.

"She is correct, *gringo*. But I am the leader and I take orders from nobody." His teeth showed white in the firelight, displayed in an expression which could be either a grin or a grimace. "Nor do I share money with anybody but my own men. You will get the fifty thousand dollars from Kane Worthington, *gringo*. And you will bring it to La Hondonada at the time I said. You will do this, or I will kill the *damisela*." Another snap of finger and thumb. "Like that. I think, perhaps, that she means even less to you than to me, *gringo*. But money, that means as much to you as to me. You have ridden far and taken a great risk to obtain money. And how much to get for your trouble—the amount you charge Kane Worthington—is your own affair. I require only fifty thousand dollars. You will go to get that for me. Now."

Edge held up the Colt and the Winchester and said, "Obliged," as he slid the revolver into its holster and canted the rifle to his shoulder. Then glanced at Nino to say, "A warning for you, kid. You ever point a gun at me again, try to kill me before I kill you. Two times is one too many."

"*Amo,* I think—" Nino began to snarl.

"Put the gun away and join the feast, *muchacho,*" Satanas invited amicably, and waved his cigar toward the dead man. "You have done well and now you are

33

one of us. You see, I have made a place for you at our table."

Nino's thin, acne-scarred face lit with delight as he hurried to the far side of the table and started to haul Ricardo off the chair.

"A favor, *gringo*," Satanas said to Edge as the half-breed made to turn away. "In the town of Indian Hill there is a doctor. His name is Laurie."

"If you say so, feller."

Satanas massaged his forehead. And snarled, "I say so. You will bring me something from him for *el dolor de cabeza*. For the headache, uh?"

"I'll see what I can do feller."

"*Amo*, what am I to do with Ricardo?" Nino called as he dragged the corpse away from the table and cast a new gloom over the celebration feast just as the sounds of merry-making were beginning to be raised again.

"Bury him, *estúpido*!" Satanas snapped. Then sighed and tapped his forehead as he muttered to Edge, "I have to think of everything for everybody. It is no wonder I always have the pain here, uh *gringo*?"

Since the half-breed was aware of the Mexican's excellent knowledge of English and had witnessed his abrupt changes from amiability to vicious brutality, he started away from the man and merely murmured, "Yeah, feller. I notice you're real sick in the head."

CHAPTER FOUR

EDGE had sweated a great deal while he was at the camp of Satanas, and, as he moved out of the range of the blazing fire, the cold night air of the Sierra Madres chilled the salty moisture on his flesh. Tension continued to ooze sweat beads from his pores while he was walking slowly across the canyon floor and then as he climbed the narrow pathway to the rim. For, although he could hear the bandit chief contributing as much as anyone to the swelling noise of the feast, he was aware of the possibility that the cunning and sometimes mercurial Satanas might suddenly have a whim to shoot him down, or perhaps kill him as the climax to a twisted plan that had been hatched at the outset.

But the half-breed reached the safety of the high ground without incident while the eating and drinking continued. And when he looked back down into the canyon, the scene in front of the adobe building was much as it had appeared when he watched from the mesquite clump. Off to one side, the skinny Nino was working hard and fast to dig a grave for Ricardo. And there was an empty chair to the right of Satanas for Grace Worthington was still unconscious. Apart from this, it was as if time had stood still and Edge had never been seen and captured by the boy.

Not in his mind though, for the capture and his helplessness during the following stretched minutes stayed fresh and stark in Edge's mind as he returned to his horse and started the long ride back across the border. And even when time and distance dulled the remembered images, his self-anger remained as cold and solid as ever in the pit of his stomach.

He had allowed his guard to slip and a mere kid had got the drop on him, in circumstances where his life or death depended upon a man who acted on impulse. And for what? Because of an impulse of his own—to capitalize on some trouble that was not his own or even of his own making.

But he was out of it now. Had been given a chance which he did not deserve. A chance to ride away from the self-styled Devil and his bunch of killers. And whatever conscience he had left would not be troubled by thoughts of the conniving Grace Worthington and the fate he left her to face up to.

His pride would not allow such a course of action, though. Only once before had he set out to do something and been forced to admit defeat—to surrender to his destiny. In everything else he had to do, he succeeded. Not always totally, but never did he fail entirely.

So, as he rode slowly along the floor of La Hondonada and clear of the northern end he heeled the gelding to a faster pace, determined to ease the self-anger that felt like an icy ball in his belly. His mind resolutely set upon being paid for the trouble he had taken—in money and in something less tangible than hard cash.

"Get up there, feller," he rasped to the horse as he demanded a gallop. "I figure I have to beat the Devil."

Bright moonlight showed him the way ahead, back to the meeting of the trails where old bloodstains on the dusty ground showed the places where two men had died. Then he made a turn, to ride along the west trail in the direction Benteen had pointed out as the way to the town of Indian Hill.

It was not much of a town. Similar to countless other settlements which Edge had passed through all over the southwestern territories. A main street perhaps a half-mile in length with two shorter side streets twisting off to the north for a few hundred feet before they became open trails flanked by small farmsteads.

A marker proclaimed the name of the town and claimed it had five hundred citizens. Maybe the figure had once been correct but as Edge slowed his horse to ride between the darkened façades of timber, adobe and brick buildings, he saw that many of them were empty and in various stages of dereliction. Houses and business premises both, abandoned to the ravages of the elements. Paint was peeled and blistered, timbers were warped, masonry was crumbled and windows were smashed. While, here and there, fires had raged and just the blackened shells of roofless walls remained.

In the places that were still occupied, and kept in a reasonable state of repair, the remaining citizenry of Indian Hill were asleep in back of darkened windows and locked doors, making the most of what was left of the night before a new day dawned. And Edge did not wake anyone as he halted his gelding in front of the Arizona Star Saloon, slid from the saddle, hitched the reins to the rail and sat down on the stoop step.

He rolled and lit a cigarette, then smoked it without taking it from his lips, hat pulled low over his forehead, shoulders hunched under his coat and hands thrust into the pockets. Feeling his flesh become as cold as the anger inside him. Then, after the cigarette was smoked, he occasionally took his hands from his pockets to cup them around his mouth and blow into the palms. He sat for over an hour like this, back resting against a stoop upright, before the light of the false dawn streaked the eastern sky and somewhere out to the north some cocks began to crow.

It was a bad way to spend the time, but it was a match for the mood of the half-breed. And it served a purpose for, when he saw the first person he had come across since leaving the camp of the Mexican bandits, he was able to greet him with an even-toned, "Morning to you."

"It's mornin' sure enough, mister," the man answered dully. "But you did right not to say it was good. Not this mornin' ain't."

"It could've been worse," Edge countered, getting to his feet and flexing his stiffened limbs.

"Matter of opinion," the thin, stoop-shouldered, sixty-or-so-years-old man growled as he drew level with Edge and halted, peered short-sightedly at the half-breed. "Ain't lookin' to earn a few bucks, are you?"

"No, feller. A lot of them."

The man, who was dressed in dungarees and an old army forage cap shook his head. "Grave diggin' don't pay high. I got two to get ready by ten."

"Need to get to the Worthington spread. Which way is that?"

The grave-digger pursed his lips and vented a low whistle. "Bad place to go today, mister. It's on account of that Grace Worthington I got the graves to dig. Stage from Tucson got held up and some Mexicans too—"

"You got work to do and I have an appointment to make, feller." Edge cut in as he unhitched the gelding's reins from the rail. "I just asked the one question."

The grave-digger sucked some saliva up from his throat and sent it in a stream to the hard-packed dirt of the street. "Reckon you'll fit in well out at the Bar-W, mister. Never have heard a friendly word from anyone who works that spread."

Edge swung up into the saddle and gazed coldly down at the man, who scowled as he supplied,

"Head out on the west trail. You'll come to a stand of timber and a creek. Spur goes off to the right to take you around the hill. You'll know when you're on Kane Worthington property."

The half-breed touched the brim of his hat and said, "Obliged."

"You're welcome, mister. Which you won't be at the Bar-W."

"You sound like you've been eating grapes before they got ripe, feller."

"Maybe I done that, mister," the man growled as he

38

turned to continue toward the church and its small, walled graveyard at the eastern end of the street. "But I ain't ever had to lower myself to eat crow on account of Worthington money."

"Better the ballyache than the indigestion, I guess," Edge agreed softly as he heeled the gelding in the opposite direction.

The grayness of dawn had driven the blackness of night from the sky now and in its somber light the town of Indian Hill presented a sorrier façade than when the half-breed had first seen it. Once it had been a thriving community—or, at least, had had the potential. For a wide variety of businesses had been established. Three banks, a dozen stores stocking both essentials and luxuries, a newspaper, two saloons and a cantina, a stage depot, a theatre, a courthouse and two office buildings with space for many shingles on the boards out front. All these on the main thoroughfare, while the side streets were lined by a mixture of hotels and private and boarding houses.

The Arizona Star Saloon, a grocery and hardware store, the stage depot, a bank and a small section of one of the office buildings were still in business. And a few of the house chimneys gave off smoke as Edge rode out of town. Fires had also been lit in the stoves of three of the dozen homesteads spread across the hill slope that rose to the north of the town. Weed-choked fields and fallen fences evidence that the rest of the place had been abandoned.

The smoke from the stacks rose lethargically into the brightening sky, as if infected by the obvious depression of the dying community from whence it came.

When the sun rose, shafting over the ridges behind him, the slow-riding Edge did not look back to see if the warmth and bright light caused Indian Hill to create a more inviting impression. He merely relished the effect it had on him—easing away the coldness of night that had seemed to penetrate his clothing and flesh to reach deep into his bones.

By the time he reached the fork in the trail and steered the horse along the spur which followed the course of a muddy creek, he was warm enough to take off his topcoat and drape it over his bedroll.

The spur and the creek—the latter widening and deepening by the yard—took a meandering course around the base of the rocky high ground for which, presumably, the town on the south side was named. Then both straightened out on the fringe of a wood of mixed timber, where the trail ran under a rustic arch constructed of pine trunks. Along the top bar of the arch the name WORTHINGTON was emblazoned in letters three feet high formed with untreated tree branches. To one side of the arch was a board warning in white painted lettering: *Private property. No admittance except by prior appointment. By order of Kane Worthington.*

The gelding had carried the half-breed no more than a few feet on to the forbidden spread when a man growled, "Can't you read, stranger?"

The man who spoke, and another one, stepped from the trees to the left of the trail. Both were in their late twenties or early thirties. Tall, broadly built, hard-faced and cold-eyed men with sun-burnished skin. Dressed like cowpunchers, they had never worked cattle in their unsullied check shirts and denim pants; their spurs were polished and their white Stetsons had no sweat stains. The Frontier Colts in their holsters and the Winchester rifles they held across the front of their bodies were a match for their crisply turned-out appearance. Each wore a shiny tin star on the left shirt-pocket.

Edge reined in the gelding and eyed the men bleakly over twenty feet, he out in the sunlight and they shaded by the timber.

"The town law is a whole lot smarter than the town," he said.

"We work for Mr. Worthington, not Chuck Meyers," the one with a dimpled chin growled.

"We ain't here to give out information, Warren!" the

deputy with a stiff right leg said in an even harsher tone. "I asked you a question, stranger!"

"I read as well as I count, feller."

The lame man nodded curtly. "That's good. So you know what the sign says. And you'll know when I get to five. By which time you'll have backed off the Bar-W property or you'll be hurtin'. One . . . two . . . "

"Somebody else is counting right now, feller," Edge put in evenly. "On me. Getting to talk with Kane Worthington. A woman who ought never to have been named Grace."

"Talk from the other side of the property line, stranger! Three . . ."

"Hey, Larry, I think we oughta listen to this guy," Warren said anxiously.

"Try to kill me, feller," the half-breed added, and continued to appear relaxed in the saddle while beneath the surface he readied himself to meet the threat. "If all you do is make me hurt, you've got two seconds to live."

"I don't take that kinda talk from any—" Larry barked.

"Wylie!" a woman shrieked.

If the man with the lame right leg heard her, he paid no attention. For his mind was set upon punishing the even-voiced, casual-looking intruder who had threatened him and was closed to any outside influence.

He turned his body from the waist rather than swung the rifle—thumb-cocking the hammer away from a breech into which a shell had already been levered.

Edge moved just his right arm, to streak his hand from the saddlehorn to the butt of the Colt jutting from his holster. And he drew, cocked, leveled and fired the revolver in a series of smooth actions which merged into a single continuous move. His eyes blinked just the once, at the crack of the bullet leaving the muzzle.

Birds took to frightened flight from among the trees as Edge, eyes merely slits of glinting blue, ignored the crumpling corpse of Larry Wylie and gazed at Warren.

41

"You didn't have to kill him," the surviving deputy groaned, shifting his horrified gaze from the body to the impassive face of the half-breed.

"Try never to break my word, feller. I told him I'd do it. So I did."

"Put your gun away this instant!" the woman snapped as she emerged from the timber on the creek side of the trail.

She was breathless from running and beads of sweat stood out on her exertion-reddened, plain face. About thirty-five, she was close to six feet tall and extremely thin, the under-played curves of her hips and breasts contoured a severely styled, high-necked, long-sleeved and narrow skirted black gown. Just the red tint of her close-cropped hair and the subtle shade of green of her eyes hinted of a blood relationship with Grace Worthington.

"This gunslinger just shot and killed Larry, Miss May," Warren complained to Grace's older and plainer sister.

"Doubtless Mr. Wylie asked for what he got," the woman countered, patting at her damp face with a handkerchief. "He spent his entire life riling people. State your business here, sir."

Edge uncocked the Colt and slid it into his holster. Then touched the brim of his hat as he answered, "Need to see your father, lady."

"Need, sir? Or want?"

"He says it's to do with Miss Grace, ma'am," Warren offered. From where he was down on his haunches beside the corpse, having checked that the bullet in Wylie's chest had in fact killed the man.

May, recovered from her hasty advance on the scene of the killing, was abruptly disconcerted again. "Then why on earth was he not admitted immediately?" she demanded.

"Mr. Worthington's orders, ma'am," Warren replied, sure that his defense was valid. "He said to allow no one through just like always."

"The damn fool," May countered, speaking aloud her thoughts. But not perturbed when she realized she had voiced her feelings. To Edge she said, "I'll bring my horse, sir. We'll ride together."

As she made to turn into the trees, Warren blurted, "What'll I do about Larry, Miss May?"

"It's the living who concern me!" the woman snorted. Then sighed in exasperation as she saw a look of helplessness grip the no-long-hardset face of the deputy. And there was something akin to pity in her voice and expression when she added, "Of course, Warren, you are still alive. I'll tell them what's happened and have someone sent down."

Then she went from sight into the deep shade among the timber.

"God, mister, I don't think I've ever seen a faster draw than that," Warren said with a shake of his head as the half-breed heeled his horse forward.

"You saw it?" Edge responded with mock surprise.

"I'll say I did."

Edge made a clucking sound with his tongue against the back of his teeth. "Then I guess I must be slowing down, feller."

"Miss May said to wait," Warren called as the half-breed rode slowly by him.

"Some women are worth waiting for, feller. She looks the kind who's used to chasing after a man."

CHAPTER FIVE

MAY Worthington rode side-saddle in her narrow skirted dress and she did it expertly, catching up with the half-breed at a gallop as he halted his gelding on the north fringe of the timber.

"I told you to wait for me, sir!" she snapped angrily as she brought her big black stallion to a stop beside the gelding. Her fists remained tightly clenched to the reins and a quirt while she glared at the impassive profile of the unshaven Edge.

"What it sounded like to me, ma'am," he replied, lighting the cigarette he had rolled while riding through the trees. "If you'd asked, maybe I would've."

He sensed her glaring anger rise still further, then subside, as he gazed out along the broad, shallow valley that stretched away toward the north-east. The gentle slopes to either side were rocky and barren of anything except for cactus, stunted pine trees and brown brush. But down on the floor there was a strip of verdant country some three miles wide by at least ten long which was watered by the creek. Lush, rolling meadows featured with extensive stands of timber: here and there a rock outcrop. At regular intervals, irrigation ditches had been dug to carry water from the creek to the bottoms of the grades which enclosed the valley.

At this end of the valley, at least two thousand head of mixed breed cattle were grazing the pastures. Further away and land was sub-divided by neat fencing into ten-acre farmsteads. The fields were well tended and the houses of the tenant farmers looked to be in a good state of repair. Luxurious, maybe, compared with the kind of places the homesteaders of Indian Hill ran. But hovels relative to the Bar-W ranch house.

"Impressive, isn't it?" the plain-faced woman said.

The house was about a mile distant from where Edge and May Worthington sat their horses. And below them, so they had a bird's-eye view of the Colonial-style mansion and its out-buildings constructed of white stone under green tile roofs. The buildings were sited in the center of an extensive stand of mixed timber which had been landscaped to form a garden of lawns and flowerbeds and ornamental pools.

"Money always impresses me, ma'am," Edge answered.

"And you're here to get some of it?"

They started their horses forward, down the sloping trail that veered away from the creek.

"Have some business to do with your father."

"Concerning the abduction of my sister."

"Right."

"You're the man Cyrus Benteen spoke of. You were at the scene of the abduction. You didn't give your name."

"Edge."

"Just Edge? Nothing else?"

"It's enough."

"My father is not an easy man to do business with, Mr. Edge. He trusts nobody."

He sensed that she was gazing fixedly at him and he looked at her. Saw there was curiosity in her green eyes—and something else. Which she displayed more blatantly as she held the level gaze of his narrowed eyes. A brand of wanton lust by a woman for a man.

He revealed no response to this as he answered, "Easy-going people don't get this rich, ma'am."

"You don't look to be rich."

Edge dropped his cigarette to the trail. "Mostly I have enough for my needs. Seldom have any wants."

She grimaced. "Then you're a very lucky man."

He didn't reply and after a few moments she shifted her gaze away from him. And asked. "I don't suppose you'll tell me about Grace?"

"You don't sound as if you care very much."

"It's been said that I'm even harder than my father," she answered and there was something akin to pride in her tone.

They were on level ground now, closing with a point on the trail where a gravel-surfaced spur veered off toward the trees which now concealed the big house.

"You like men so much you've got nothing left for your family, ma'am?"

He expected an angry rebuttal. Instead, she laughed and it was an identical sound to the peals of laughter he had heard uttered by her younger sister at the bandit camp across the border before Grace Worthington realized what kind of trouble she was in. "I'm as transparent as glass where that's concerned, aren't I?" She laughed again. "And it doesn't shock you, I like that."

They turned onto the spur and the hooves of the horses crunched gravel.

"But then, it would take an awful lot to shock a man like you, I guess?"

They rode through the trees and then between the neatly trimmed lawns featured with symmetrical flowerbeds and many-shaped pools. While the woman remained at ease with the silence—seemed to be enjoying the lack of responses from the half-breed. As they approached a large half-circle of gravel which stretched from one corner to the other of the house façade, she steered her horse to the side.

"I'll instruct the help to do something about poor Larry Wylie, Mr. Edge. Father is going to be awfully mad about you shooting him."

"Just one thing after another for him," the half-breed answered. "But I figure he's used to that."

"I'll see you in a while, I hope," the plainer of the Worthington daughters said as she used the quirt to demand a canter from the big stallion and rode from sight through a gateway into a walled courtyard at the rear of the house.

This as Edge reined in his horse, swung down from the saddle and led the animal to a hitching-rail at one side of the mansion's column-flanked porch. He felt weary—apart from the brief rest on the saloon stoop in the cold, early-morning hours he had not slept for more than a day and a night—and this probably had much to do with his susceptibility to the odd feeling of unreality that suffused him.

He had first become aware of this sensation of being in a kind of waking dream when he had looked down from the head of the valley on to the totally unexpected scene spread before him. He was in the Territory of Arizona, just one hill away from a grim and destitute settlement where the people had to scratch for a survival living from the arid and unproductive soil. And yet here it was as if a great stretch of Oregon had been miraculously lifted from its roots and set down in the surrounding near-wilderness. Then, to compound the strangeness of the setting, there was the Worthington house which would have seemed unremarkable in the Virginias or the Carolinas but which was completely out of context in the south-west. Finally, to set the seal on the hallucinatory quality which had insinuated itself into the mind of the normally unimaginative half-breed there was the woman. Who seemed to care nothing about the fate of her abducted sister, was unaffected by sudden and violent death and had made it as plain as her face that she was available if he wanted her.

"Shit," he growled softly as he stepped up onto the porch and yanked on a velvet rope that rang a bell inside the house. "You've caught a touch of money-fever is all."

The porch, the columns and the brass-studded door were all white, brilliantly so in the early morning sunlight. And as he waited for the bell to be answered, he was conscious of his dusty clothing and his unwashed and unshaven face.

48

The man who opened the door snapped, "How the frig did you get here?"

What he wore was a perfect match with the garb of Wylie and Warren, complete to the deputy's badge on the left pocket of his shirt. He did not have a Winchester.

Edge spat between the two pillars on the right of the porch and used the arrogant toughness of the man to lever himself back to harsh reality.

"I killed a man," he growled. And drew, cocked and leveled the Colt. "He looked a lot like you, feller. If it's the way it has to be, I'm ready to supply the local mortician with a matching pair."

"You can't—" the neatly dressed deputy started.

He held his ground as the half-breed stepped across the threshold, as his eyes, showing surprise rather than fear, shifted from the gun aimed at his belly to the glittering gaze of Edge. So he failed to see the intruder's left hand bunch into a fist, but felt the punch impact with his abdomen, as a rush of air from his throat curtailed his protest. Then he doubled over and groaned in response to a blow from the Colt muzzle against the nape of his neck. And collapsed to the threshold.

"Seems I can," Edge muttered, sliding the gun back into the holster as he stepped over the unconscious form of the deputy.

"Ralph, who is it?" a man called, sounding as if he had a short temper on a shorter leash.

The half-breed glanced around the large, two-storey-high entrance hall which had oil paintings hung on the walls, thick carpet spread on the floor and a double, curved staircase rising to a balcony at the rear. Many doors led off it and the impatient man was in a room to the right, where the door was ajar.

Edge could not close the front door without moving Ralph and he wasted neither time nor effort before angling across the hall, his footfalls making hardly any sound on the rich pile carpet. Close to the partially

49

open doorway he had to swing around a large, winged chair where Ralph had been seated, the upholstery still showing the indentation of his butt and an old Tucson newspaper draped over an arm.

"Ralph, I asked you a question, damnit!"

"Name's Edge, Mr. Worthington." The half-breed swung the door gently open as he supplied the information, stepped into the room and closed it behind him. "Ralph's temporarily indisposed. Not like another of your hands, feller. Wylie's dead. You're a hard man to get to see."

Kane Worthington was shocked by the unexpected appearance of Edge and by the words he spoke with a total lack of any emotion. And the man seated behind the big oak desk was not used to being surprised— seemed for stretched seconds to be diminished in stature by his unfamiliar state of experiencing utter helplessness. But he fought it and had his composure firmly back in place just a moment before a trembling fit was about to shake his very fiber. And just his hands shook, as he snatched them off the desk top and dropped them out of sight.

He was in his early fifties, close to six feet tall and with a well-built frame on the verge of running from solid flesh to fat. He still had a lot of hair atop his squarish head, which had for the most part grayed from its original auburn color. The flesh of his handsome face was deeply lined and stained dark brown by the elements. His eyes were of the same pale shade of green as those of his daughters.

He wore the pants of a suit, a matching vest, a white shirt and a string tie. The clothing was crumpled and his face was haggard with weariness.

"You're a dead man, Edge!" Worthington rasped through teeth clenched to a pipe-stem. "You'll be tried, convicted and hanged for murder!"

His shirt and vest-front were marked by smears of gray tobacco ash, and brown juice had stained his bris-

50

tled jaw. He looked like a man who had been up all night.

"Man's supposed to be innocent until proved guilty, feller," the half-breed answered as he crossed to the desk.

The room was a study, furnished as expensively as the entrance hall. The wood of the furniture was all dark oak, the upholstery was of polished brown leather and the carpet looked like a high-priced import from the Orient. The books in the floor-to-ceiling, glass-fronted cases which lined every wall had a brand-new, unopened appearance.

Worthington felt composed enough to bring his hands into view—clenched them into big fists as he rested them on the desk top. Then he raised them and slammed them hard down as he glared angrily up into the glittering slits of the intruder's eyes.

"Don't you answer me back in my own house, you crook!" he snarled. He made to rise from his chair, and winced as his stiffened joints protested the move. Then he gasped as Edge leaned across the desk, placed a clawed hand to the top of his head and shoved him hard—to jolt him back down into his chair.

"Listen, feller," the half-breed rasped, his lips hardly moving as he remained bent over the desk, his face no more than six inches from that of Worthington, and his eyes narrowed almost entirely closed against the bright sunlight that shafted into the smoke-layered room from the three tall windows in back of where the older man sat. "I've gone to a lot of trouble on account of the Worthington family. I've ridden a lot of miles, lost a lot of sleep and twice I could've been killed. And I don't invite that kind of trouble unless there's a reward at the end of it. So you owe me, feller. And I aim to collect. But you got a choice. You can pay me or I can take. Taking'll cause me more trouble and I figure that's worth a bonus. Won't cost you any more cash though. I'll just beat the hell out of you. Which, the way I'm

51

feeling now, will be worth more than anything every cent you have could buy me."

There was a chair at either front corner of the desk and Edge straightened up, backed to the one on the left and turned it slightly before he dropped wearily into it. From its new position could see Worthington, the three windows and the door by just swinging his eyes along their narrowed sockets.

Kane Worthington had not been afraid of Edge. After an initial grimace of pain as he was thudded back into his chair, he had held the cold, glittering gaze steadily without revealing any hint of his feeling about the physical attack and rasping threat of worse to come. Now, his hand steady, he removed the pipe from his teeth and knocked out smoking ash into a porcelain dish already heaped with the remains of many smokes.

"Cyrus Benteen is a fool," he said levelly. "And because of that, I owe you an apology, Mr. Edge."

"A man can't feed himself and his horse on apologies, feller. You owe me two thousand dollars. A Mexican who calls himself Satanas wants fifty thousand."

Worthington grimaced twice—once as each figure was mentioned. Then seemed to ignore what had been said as he continued, "Benteen told me you were a run-of-the-mill saddlebum with a lot of greed but no guts. That you stood by and watched the stage held up and only showed any interest when you were told I was rich."

Edge sighed. "He told you the truth about what happened. I don't give a shit about what he thinks of me. For two thousand I'll deliver the ransom money and buy your daughter back from the Mexicans."

Knuckles rapped on the door. "Father, is Edge with—"

A gasp curtailed what May Worthington was calling and the door was flung open. And Ralph lunged into the room, came to a swaying halt with his hand fisted around his holstered Colt when he saw his boss and the half-breed seated quietly at the desk.

"Boss, I was—" Ralph began, anger and confusion struggling for command of his features while, in back of him, the plain-faced woman smiled her enjoyment of the situation.

"You were lucky, deputy," her father cut in grimly. "Your incompetence cost you a couple of bruises maybe. I understand Larry Wylie paid with his life."

"I've sent Joel and Noah to bring in Wylie's body, Father," May said.

"Get back to your post, Ralph," Kane Worthington ordered. "May, have the kitchen bring some coffee. Except when it comes, I do not wish to be disturbed."

The deputy, now showing blatant resentment, backed out of the room. But May stepped inside, tight-lipped then rasping, "He can go to the kitchen. I want to hear about Grace."

She slammed the door in Ralph's face.

Her father snarled, "You'll do like I damn well tell you, girl!"

"Or you'll spank me?" she taunted, striding across the room and dropping into the chair at the desk Edge had left vacant. She smelled of fresh morning air, horse sweat and stable. In pleasant contrast to the stale tobacco smoke and the rancid odor of the half-breed's unwashed body and clothing. Determination showed on her features again, "I want to know about Grace."

Now her father became taunting in his tone and expression as he sneered, "Sisterly love all of a sudden, girl?"

Edge was looking out of one of the tall windows at a flat-bed wagon heading down the gravel driveway with two men up on the seat. He vented a grunt of impatience and when the father and daughter looked at him, said, "Do you love her fifty-two thousand dollars worth or not, Mr. Worthington?"

The woman shook her head. "That's not the question, Edge. Question is, how much does he value his pride."

53

"Didn't ask you a damn thing, lady," Edge growled.

Worthington thudded just one fist on the desk top this time. And sighed deeply as he quelled his anger for May so that he could speak levelly to the half-breed. "I'm willing to pay every cent I have if that's what it takes to get Grace away from those kidnapping bastards." Then unconsciously imitated a characteristic gesture of Satanas by clicking his thumb and little finger. "But I won't pay one cent just like that."

Edge nodded and got to his feet. And this move sprang deep concern into the eyes of the man across the desk. "I guess there's still a place in that near ghost town where I can bed down for a few hours?"

Now Worthington was curious as he nodded.

"It's been a long night after a long day and I need to sleep a while," the half-breed went on. "The money has to be at a place about four hours' ride from here by noon tomorrow. Why you pay the money makes no difference to me. Just need to know if you're going to pay. When you've decided that, you let me know. And you have the money ready in good time. Won't need my part of it until after the deal has been made with the Mexicans."

"You don't have to stay in town," May said quickly. "There are plenty of spare rooms in this place."

"The girl's right," her father added. "And you'll be far more comfortable here in the house than anywhere at Indian Hill."

Edge halted halfway to the door, not liking the idea of staying in this rich house where money had so obviously failed to buy happiness, but relishing even less the prospect of riding back to the grim town beyond the hill at the head of the valley.

"You'll have my horse taken care of?"

"Of course," Kane Worthington assured. "We have fine stables here."

Edge nodded. "Show me where I sleep and have someone wake me at noon."

"I'll do it," May offered, getting hurriedly to her feet.

"We'll talk when you've rested," her father told Edge as the half-breed reached the door and opened it, his voice suddenly very thick with a bone-deep weariness of his own. "I have a great deal to do."

May made to leave the room ahead of Edge, but he stepped across the threshold first, as Ralph rose from the armchair and glared menacingly at him.

"Your manners leave much to be desired, sir!" the woman accused acidly.

"Like this family, lady," he countered as she closed the door.

A young and slimly pretty Negress came across the hall, carrying a silver tray set with a silver coffee pot and bone china cups, saucers, milk jug and sugar bowl. She was suddenly frightened and looked helplessly at May and Ralph when Edge blocked her path and took the pot and a cup from the tray.

"Obliged," he told the girl.

"It's all right, Rose," May Worthington said. "This *gentleman* is not familiar with our ways. Please fetch another pot for Mr. Kane." She pointed to the stairway. "The guest rooms are on the upper floor, Mr. Edge."

"He's staying here?" Ralph growled as the Negress turned to head back for the kitchen.

"Yes. His horse is out front. Take it around to the stables."

"I ain't a—" Ralph started.

May stamped her foot. "You're one of the help and you'll do as you're told!" she snapped.

Red-faced wih the anger of humiliation, Ralph whirled and strode toward the front door, muttering under his breath. He slammed the door behind him as May took fast, mincing steps—speed hampered by the narrowness of her skirt—to catch up with Edge who was almost at the top of the stairs. She turned left to lead him along a broad landing off the railed balcony.

"Kindly walk this way and do your best to act like a

gentleman while you are in this house," she instructed tightly.

Edge fell in behind her and expressed a wry, fleeting smile as he drawled, "If I could walk that way, lady I don't figure I'd be any kind of man."

CHAPTER SIX

THE room into which the woman ushered Edge was at the rear of the house. It was large and as expensively furnished with good taste as every other part of the Worthington home he had seen. The view from the lace-curtain-hung window was down into the walled courtyard and the timber beyond which screened all but the crests of the rises which enclosed the rich valley outside the immediate vicinity of the house.

Edge poured coffee into the small cup and drank it at a swallow as he stood at the window and watched Ralph lead the gelding into the stable.

The door closed and he was not aware May was still in the room until she spoke.

"I can have the help bring a tub and hot water, Edge. Or arrange anything else you need to make you comfortable."

The hardness had left her voice and Edge detected a brand of coy invitation in the tone she used, then saw it blatantly displayed when he turned from the window. For there was a smile on her plain face which was at once eager and gentle, and she stood against the door in an attitude which displayed her slim body to the best advantage.

"You mean you'll be happy to have me screw you, lady?" he asked evenly.

She was disconcerted for just a second. Then she vented a throaty laugh. "I should have expected you to say something like that, Edge. You being the kind of

57

man you are. Not the kind to waste time beating about the bush."

She came further into the room and sat on the side of the big double bed as the half-breed poured more coffee into the small cup. He remained with his back to the window.

"Seems like you people figure you have all the time in the world to waste, lady."

She leaned back and half lay against the headboard of the bed, her eyes puzzled.

"No one seems to give a shit about what kind of trouble your sister is in."

She laughed again, and Edge experienced a stab of cold anger as he realized she was laughing at him. She saw the dangerous glint in his slitted eyes under the hatbrim and curtailed her mirth, swung her feet up onto the bed, raised her knees and hugged them to her small breasts.

"I'm sorry, Edge. You're a complete stranger here and can't be expected to understand the kind of situation you've entered. Do you want me to explain?"

He moved from the window to sit in a basketweave chair and used the toe of each foot to ease off his boots. The need to sleep was becoming more urgent with each moment and as his weariness increased, so the strange quality of unreality enclosed him more tightly. He emptied the cup a second time and tilted the pot to refill it.

"If you can tell it all before I've finished this."

"One word sums it up," she said. "Money. This house and the whole valley was built and made with money. And it exists for the sole purpose of making more money."

"I'm through with first-grade learning, lady," Edge interrupted. "There are some things I can figure out for myself."

"Money buys a great many things," she went on as if he had not made any comment. "You know that, of course, and you can see all around you that Worthington money has paid for a lot of creature comforts. But

58

all this is of little importance to my father, Edge. Had it not been for my late mother he would have been content to live in a hole in the ground and spent every cent that came his way on buying the only thing that does interest him. Power, Edge. It's all he's ever wanted and he won't be satisfied until he's the most powerful man in creation. Which is impossible. But he doesn't think so. Because, Edge, Kane Worthington is crazy."

She paused to invite a response from the half-breed. But he merely refilled the cup to almost empty the coffee pot.

"When those Mexicans took Grace off the stage," she continued," they showed they didn't give a hoot for Worthington power. And that is what riles my father. The fact that it is a daughter who has been stolen from him is of no consequence. He would be feeling exactly as he is now if they had stolen money, a horse or a few head of cows from him. He's not angry at what Felipe Cortez did so much, as outraged that the man had the gall to do it."

Edge expressed mild and fleeting surprise—as he recalled how the bandit chief reacted each time Grace Worthington called him Felipe. And May smiled her satisfaction at drawing a show of emotion to the half-breed's face.

"Guess you haven't ever come across a man like that?" she posed.

"Your father and Cortez know each other?" Edge countered and set the record straight about the reason for his surprise.

"Yes." She shook her head, but not in contradiction of her reply. "You really are an innocent abroad, aren't you?"

"You were going to change that, lady. The coffee's almost all gone and you haven't said anything except that your pa aims to be ruler of the world and doesn't take kindly to people who spit in his eye."

She sighed. "Very well. In a nutshell. Felipe Cortez used to run the cantina in Indian Hill. Like a lot of other people had good businesses in town. Father wanted to buy up everything there, after he'd made the valley what it is. Extend his empire maybe. Call it what you like. But only a handful agreed to sell. Those that didn't, he put pressure on. The town can't exist as anything better than it is today without drawing customers from the valley. So Father forbade anyone who works on the Bar-W ranch and farms to go to town. And he had shipped in all the supplies people would normally buy in town. And sold it at a loss to undercut the Indian Hill stores.

"Offers to sell started to come in quickly then, but Father didn't take them up. The town hadn't given him what he wanted when he demanded it so he set out to punish Indian Hill. And since you rode through the town to get here, you'll have seen the result of his spite.

"Cortez was one of the first to go broke. He went south over the border, collected a bunch of other Mexicans, called himself Satanas and took to crime. He stays mostly in Mexico now. But right at the start of it, he brought his men to Indian Hill and burned down every property there that father had been able to buy.

"Chuck Meyers who's the sheriff in town couldn't or wouldn't do anything about it. And that was when father went as high as was necessary to get himself appointed a territorial marshal and hired men like Ralph Quine, Larry Wylie and Warren Hanson as deputies. There's seven more like it around the place and they've never been able to track down Cortez.

"But now there's a chance that they can. And Father intends to see that they do. He doesn't need you, Edge. But since you're around and available, he'll use you. Be warned, though. You killed Larry, beat up Ralph and virtually broke into this house. All that will be sticking in his craw and when this business about Grace is finished, he'll have the time to make you regret what you did."

Edge got up and set the empty coffee pot and cup on

60

a bureau. Said, "Obliged for the information and the warning, lady. Like to bed down now."

She swung her feet to the floor and rose from the bed, an intense expression in her pale green eyes as she watched him stretch out on top of the bedcovers.

"Listen, I have a proposition to put to you, Edge," she said in a tone to match her expression.

He tipped his hat forward to cover his face and answered as he clasped his hands at the nape of his neck, "You ain't my type, lady."

He heard her foot stamp at the carpet. "Listen. You can make much more than a measly two thousand dollars out of this. You can have it all. If you tell father that Cortez insisted you bring the money to him—on your own—you can just ride off with it."

"Leaving Grace to be murdered."

"Cortez won't kill Grace!" she came back quickly. "Because then he wouldn't have anything to bargain with. He'll just demand another fifty thousand. And Father will pay. By which time you and I will be a long way from the Bar-W. And Kane Worthington is only a tin god in this neck of the woods. Outside of Arizona— even outside of Pima County—he has no more power and influence than a sharecropper."

"Uh uh," Edge said under his hat. "Just one thing. Why should I share the bundle with you, lady?"

"It's my idea," she answered.

"Worth how much, you figure?"

"As much as you're willing to give me," she said dully. "I just need to get away from this place. Far enough away so Kane Worthington can't force me to come back again. Out of the territory would be best. Then you can go your own way alone if you like. Or maybe you'll like having me with you. I'm not blind and I'm not a fool, Edge. I know that Grace got more than her fair share of the good looks in this family and that I'm a long way short of being a raving beauty. But believe me, I know what it takes to please a man. And if you say the word I'm willing to prove that right here and now."

There was a tremor in her voice as she made the offer.

Edge's tone was harshly cold as he said, "Get your clothes off, lady."

She caught her breath and there was nervous excitement in the sound. Then he heard her shoes kicked off, her feet padding to the door and the click of the key turning in the lock. Next came a series of softer sounds—the rustle of fabric as May Worthington removed her dress and underthings and dropped them to the floor. While she undressed—standing no more than three feet from the side of the bed—she breathed deeply, as if she had to make an effort to contain a powerful excitement. Then there were long seconds of total silence before she spoke again.

"I don't consider I am too hard to look at, Edge."

He removed one hand from the nape of his neck to raise the Stetson brim and turned his head just a fraction to look at her slender nakedness. She had fine skin for a woman of her age and despite her tall and narrow build the flesh was firm rather than slack and her bones did not protrude overmuch. The small mounds of her brown-crested breasts did not sag and despite his weariness and his contempt for the woman, he experienced the beginning of arousal as his slitted eyes were drawn to the triangle of luxuriant red hair which veed at the base of her flat belly between her lithe and long legs.

He knew she was aware of this as he raked his eyes up the length of her body and saw the smile of satisfaction which parted her lips—failed to reach her eyes which were filled with lust in urgent need of fulfilment. Then anger and hatred claimed her plain features when he allowed the hat to cover his face again and said,

"Get dressed, lady. Anything that easy ain't worth having."

She tried to hurl words at him, but they were trapped in her constricted throat and emerged only as a series of startled gasps. But then she tried again and snarled, "You lousy, rotten bastard!"

A boot heel crashed against the door and it burst open. Before it banged against the wall, Edge had rolled off the bed and his right hand was fisted to the butt of his holstered Colt. He thumbed back the hammer as May Worthington screamed.

It was Ralph Quine who had broken in the door. But the deputy, hand clear of his Colt, stepped back off the threshold so that Kane Worthington could stride into the room. He did not wear a gun, and Edge eased his hammer to rest and came erect as the gray-haired rancher rasped,

"Can't you ever get enough man, you slut?"

Rage seemed to quiver every fiber of his being and the color of his face shaded from crimson to mottled purple as he halted in front of his naked daughter. She had managed to snatch up a chemise and now held it tightly to the front of her body, concealing her breasts and sex. Terror of her father's anger seemed to transfix her to the floor.

"Not content with shaming yourself and me under my own roof, you were also planning to rob me! Maybe at the expense of your sister's life!"

His arm swung and she gasped and leaned back, fearing a blow. But he simply caught hold of the chemise and ripped it from her grasp.

"Let's all see what kind of goods you were trying to trade with, girl!" Worthington snarled. And slapped away his daughter's hands as she attempted to use these to cover herself. "Though I reckon Ralph's not looking at anything he hasn't seen before! From what I've heard, there's not a man on the Bar-W who hasn't screwed that scrawny body bare-assed! Come here, girl!"

He caught hold of her right wrist and she screamed in pain as he wrenched her around, took two forward steps, sat on the side of the bed and forced her, belly down, across his thighs.

"No!" she shrieked, and tried to. writhe from his grasp. But he grasped a bunch of her hair and hooked one of his legs between hers so that she was trapped. Then he began to pound on her naked rear, each powerful crack of his hand against her flesh drawing a high-pitched wail from her gaping, spittle-run mouth.

"It's long overdue, you whore!" he roared. "It's about time you learned that men aren't just around to satisfy your demands, girl! And the next time you plan on robbing me, maybe you'll recall this and think again!"

Kane Worthington's rage held him locked in a private world where just he and his helpless victim existed. And when Edge shifted his gaze from the rapidly reddening buttocks of the woman he saw that Quine was also temporarily detached from everything except enjoyment of his own fantasy. For the deputy was staring fixedly at the punished flesh of May Worthington—his eyes bright with lust as his tongue darted constantly in and out while he breathed rapidly through his nostrils.

"Enough, feller," the half-breed said, but nobody heard the words. And the powerful barriers of strong emotions—sexual desire, blind rage and stinging pain—were not penetrated until he rounded the end of the bed and fastened a grip on Kane Worthington's arm just as the man was about to launch another blow at his daughter.

The rancher snapped his head around so hard that a bone in his neck cracked. And the anger aroused by May was abruptly directed at the half-breed. But there was less ferocity in his eyes now and his color was not so high —the interruption having taken his rage off the broil. He abruptly looked close to exhaustion and there was no bite in his voice as he growled, "This is none of your damn business, stranger."

"Say the word, sir!" Quine asked eagerly, and draped a hand over his holstered revolver.

Worthington looked toward the doorway when Edge

released his arm—and saw the final remnants of vicarious pleasure on the deputy's face.

"Get back downstairs, Ralph," he said, softly but with heavy menace.

Quine complied immediately, scowling his displeasure at the dismissal. Then May began to sob, and vented a high-pitched cry as her father stood up and she fell hard to the floor.

"You conducted yourself far better than I in this unfortunate situation, Mr. Edge," Kane Worthington said thickly as he stepped over the shaking form of his naked daughter. "It is not my custom to spy on my guests or my girls. But it is Quine's business to see that my interests are protected. May's behavior and my response to it disgusts me. I am much impressed by the way you acted. We will discuss the more important matter after you have rested."

He left the room in a manner that was as stiff and formal as the words and the tone of voice in which he spoke them.

When Edge looked down at the woman he saw she had reached for her dress and was holding it against her flesh. Her pale, tear-run face with the eyes red-rimmed was half turned toward his towering form.

"Thank you for stopping him," she whispered after gulping for breath. "In that kind of rage, he was capable of killing me."

"I did it for me, lady," the half-breed told her coldly as he lay out on the bed again. "Find it easier to sleep when things are quiet."

He shifted his hat from the pillow to his face again. And closed his eyes gratefully against the pale daylight that filtered in under the brim of the Stetson, heard the woman groan as she eased to her feet, pulled on her dress and gathered up the underthings.

"You'll live to regret throwing in your hand with Kane Worthington, Edge," she warned morosely.

"Right now, lady," the half-breed muttered, "be

obliged if you'd take note of what your pa's hand did to your butt."

"That's something I'm never likely to forget," she replied bitterly.

"Just so long as you keep it in mind until you're out of this room."

"Uh?"

Edge sighed. "Beat it, lady."

CHAPTER SEVEN

EDGE came awake to the hammering of a fist on the door. And he smelled the stink of his body and tasted the acid of old cigarettes in his mouth. As always, he had total and instant recall of where he was and the events which had led him to be here. His eyes still felt gritty with tiredness and his head was a little fuzzy—he had not slept long enough to make up for being awake almost the entire night.

But he was ready to draw, cock and fire the Colt as he knocked the hat off his face, sat up on the bed and swung his feet to the floor. Only then called out, "It ain't locked and I'm decent."

The man who swung open the door and stepped into the room was another who wore a tin star on his left shirt-pocket. But he was not one of Kane Worthington's hired deputies. He was in his late forties, about five feet ten inches tall and solidly built with just the beginning of a fleshy thickening at his belly. He had a round face with a high forehead where his dark hair had receded. A thick moustache concealed his top lip and drooped to each side of his mouth. His eyes were as narrowed as those of Edge, but their color was inky black. He was dressed in black, from head to toe: the lawman's star, the bullets in the loops of his gunbelt and the Remington revolver in his hip holster providing the only contrasts.

"You're Edge, I guess," he growled as he halted just inside the room, and hooked both his thumbs over the front of his gunbelt.

The half-breed nodded and stood up as he said, "And I figure you for the Indian Hill sheriff. Meyers."

"Right, mister. Which means we got us a bone to pick. Concernin' murder and kidnappin'."

"Way I heard it, feller," Edge said as he began to unfasten the buttons of his shirt, "you ain't usually too concerned with what Felipe Cortez and his bunch get up to."

Meyers used the back of a boot heel to kick the door closed. "I'm here to listen to the facts concernin' the abduction of Miss Grace Worthington, mister!" he snarled. "Her old man's opinion of how I carry out my duties as sheriff don't interest me one bit."

Edge dropped his shirt on the bed and peeled the upper part of his red longjohns off his torso as he went to the bureau. The livid scar-tissue of old wounds marked the dark, solidly packed flesh at his left shoulder, right hip and just below the elbow on the inside of his left arm. But Meyers found the most intriguing feature of naked-to-the-waist man to be the lower part of a narrow leather pouch that showed below the ends of the black hair between the shoulder blades. And did a double take when, after the half-breed had poured water from a pitcher into a basin on the bureau, he pulled a straight razor from the pouch.

Edge saw this reflected in the mirror which rose from tre rear of the bureau and he said, "I don't only use it for shaving, feller."

Then he put down the razor and began to wash his face, torso and arms—using a cake of soap which he found along with towels in a drawer of the bureau.

Meyers grimaced at some image this comment called to his mind. Then accused, "Seth Barrow tells me you came through town at dawn this mornin', mister."

"Guess he's the man who went to dig the graves."

"Right. And from what Cyrus Benteen said, it seemed to me you're the man that took off after the Mexicans. You should have stopped off at my place and—"

68

"Had a message for Kane Worthington, feller," Edge cut in as he began to towel his body dry. "Cortez didn't make mention of you."

Meyers frowned his anger, then sighed out of it. "All right, Edge. There ain't no point in us hasslin'. What's between Kane Worthington and me ain't no concern of yours and right now it ain't important. Main thing is that crimes have been committed in my jurisdiction and it's my job to bring in the people responsible." He paused. "And your duty to help me."

Edge lathered his face and began to shave, hardly needing to glance in the mirror as he stroked the honed blade of the razor over the flesh yet still able to preserve the even line of the underplayed Mexican-style moustache that curved down to either side of his thin lips.

"Sure, feller. Guess you know what happened when the stage was held up. After that I trailed the Mexicans and their prisoner across the border. Cortez has about twenty men and they're holed up at what looks to be an old *Federale* post in a canyon a few hours' ride from here. I got careless and I got caught. Talked my way out of it by offering to act as the go-between. The cost of getting the Worthington woman back is fifty grand. Delivered the message and now I'm waiting to hear if Kane Worthington figures his daughter is worth that much."

He toweled surplus lather off his face, wiped the razor clean and replaced it in the pouch. Then pushed his arms back into the top portion of the longjohns.

"Where's the exchange scheduled to take place? And when?"

"Another canyon that almost runs into the one where the Mexicans are camped, Sheriff. Called La Hondonada. Mexican side of the border, I figure. Outside of your jurisdiction?"

Meyers scowled. "Right. But I can get cooperation from the *Federales*."

Two clocks in the house had been striking, confusing

the number of chimes. But the short shadows in the courtyard below the window where Edge stood, buttoning his shirt, pointed up the time of noon.

"You've got twenty-four hours to fix it, Sheriff," the half-breed said. "And if you do, maybe that's as long as Grace Worthington has to live."

The hands of Chuck Meyers—the thumbs still hung over his belt—bunched into fists. But no tighter than his lips were compressed. Then, "She'll likely die anyway, mister. Kane Worthington won't hand over fifty thousand greenbacks without puttin' up a fight."

From the chair, where he sat to pull on his boots, Edge asked, "You care, feller?"

The lawman formed his lips into a line that suggested he was about to spit. But he swallowed the saliva. "About the Worthingtons, not a wooden nickel, mister. But I ain't gonna hold still and let the killin' of those two Wells Fargo men go by."

The half-breed nodded and went to the bed to put on his hat. "So we both got things to do, Sheriff. Right now I have to talk money with Worthington."

"He's already doin' that with somebody else, mister."

Edge eyed the lawman quizzically.

"At the bank in Indian Hill."

"Way I heard it, nobody in the valley ever deals with anybody in town."

"Puzzlin', ain't it?" Meyers said with a slight, mirthless smile on his lips and in his dark eyes.

The half-breed's features were impassive as he considered for a few seconds what Meyers had told him. Then, "He take all his deputies with him?"

"Deputies!" the sheriff growled and looked again as if he was ready to spit at the carpet. "Hired guns is all they are. Worthington ain't nothin' more than an honorary marshal. No, just Quine went with him. But Worthington knows better than to order his gunslingers to keep me outta the valley when I'm on law business. Understand you ran into some trouble getting into the valley, mister?"

"Seems you keep your ear to the ground," Edge said as he led the way out of the room.

"Try to. But on this occasion it was a couple of feet from Warren Hanson's mouth when he told me what happened to Larry Wylie."

They moved along the landing, across a corner of the balcony and down one of the arms of the curving staircase.

"And May Worthington wasn't exactly what you'd call whisperin' when she backed up what Hanson said."

"They make it out to be murder?" Edge asked as they reached the hallway.

"The cold-blooded shootin' down of a man as innocent as a baby just outta the womb."

The front door of the house was open and they passed over the threshold and paused on the sunlit porch, eyes narrowed against the glare off the whitened columns and step.

"Came on too strong, uh?"

"Right. Hanson I can understand. Him bein' in the same line of work and a buddy of Wylie. But May . . . well, I ain't never heard her say a bad word against anyone in pants—except for her pa, of course."

Edge parted his lips to show a wry smile. "Figure that was the trouble, Sheriff. I was in them and wouldn't get out of them."

There was plain-to-see mirth in the brief smile which came and went from Meyers' face. "Well, I sure enough understand her attitude now, mister." He stepped down from the porch, went to where his horse was hitched to the rail and swung up into the saddle. "I'm grateful for you telling me about everythin', Edge. New experience for me—gettin' co-operation from somebody on the Bar-W payroll."

"Just on Bar-W property, feller. Not the payroll."

Chuck Meyers leaned forward in the saddle to reach out and pull the reins free of the rail. And the move probably saved his life. For the bullet rifled through thin air no more than an inch away from the curve of

71

his stooped back. And part of a second later the crack of the gunshot sounded simultaneously with the shattering glass of a house window.

The lawman powered out of the saddle instinctively, hit the gravel hard with a grunt of pain and lunged on all fours for the cover of the porch. This as his horse reared, turned and bolted. And Edge dropped into a crouch, drew and cocked his Colt, snapped his head to the side to look in the direction from which the rifle had been fired.

He saw a smooth lawn encircling a sun-glinting pool and beyond—perhaps a hundred feet away—the impenetrable cover of thick timber.

"Sonofabitch!" Meyers said hoarsely as he scampered up the step to the porch. Then threw himself flat to the whitened cement when a second shot cracked.

The half-breed had already flung himself backwards across the threshold by then—having seen the white puff of muzzle smoke which signaled the approach of the second bullet.

Dust and chips of carved stone flew away from one of the porch pillars at a point which showed the sharpshooter was aiming at Edge.

Men shouted as Meyers bellied in through the doorway and Edge came up on his haunches to peer around the frame. But the voices were raised in back of the house. From the area of timber where the shots had been fired, there was just solid silence for extended seconds. Then a yell of encouragement and the thud of hooves on turf.

Edge powered upright and lunged forward, was aware of more shouts and the crunch of gravel under footfalls behind him as he pounded toward the spot where the sniper had been positioned.

"Not him, you damn fools!" Meyers snarled at the group of a half-dozen Bar-W men rounded the corner of the house and made to draw guns against the apparently retreating half-breed.

Then the lawman gave chase.

Edge plunged into the timber and then had to swerve to left and right around the tree trunks. Did not come clear on the other side of the encircling stand until the galloping hoofbeats had faded from earshot. And he came to a halt, aware that without a horse of his own, he had no chance of catching the man who had tried to kill Meyers and himself. For the broad valley had a convoluted bottom and now that the rifleman was out of sight, he could stay hidden for its entire length, provided he took his time and followed a tortuous course that kept high ground and rock outcrops, stands of timber and clumps of brush between himself and those who searched for him.

The half-breed had the Colt back in its holster and was breathing easily again when the breathless Meyers reached him, mopping sweat from his high forehead with a kerchief.

"The bushwhacker got away, uh?" the lawman gasped.

"Sure did," Edge answered tightly, almost concealing the anger he felt at having been shot at, as the glinting slits of his eyes continued to survey the lush terrain of the valley bottom. Realizing that the man was probably down off his horse now—leading the animal by the reins so that he would not make much noise and could hear more easily the sounds of pursuit.

The Bar-W men made plenty of noise as they came through the timber. Warren Hanson and two more men wearing deputy badges, plus a Negro who smelled of horses and two cowpunchers wearing chaps, gloves and spurs.

"What happened?" one of the men with a badge on his shirt asked.

"A guy took a couple of shots at us, Craven," Meyers answered sourly. And his expression matched his tone as he raked his eyes over the hard faces of the trio of deputies. "Seems like Worthington is throwin' good money after bad keepin' you men on the payroll. People ain't safe just walkin' in and outta the house."

73

"Go to hell, Meyers! Mr. Worthington pays us to protect him and what's his is all."

Out in the open, the sheriff did not hold back from spitting. "Seems your boss got just the badges from Tucson, Kahn. Must have forgot to order the book of rules that sets out the duties and responsibilities of a deputy marshal."

"You ain't got no room to talk, Sheriff!" Hanson countered, shifting his glowering eyes from Edge to Meyers. "Seein' as how you're so damn buddy-buddy with a murderer who oughta be locked up in the jailhouse!"

"I better get back to makin' them horseshoes for you guys," the Negro muttered nervously, and retreated into the trees.

The two cowpunchers took their cue and followed him.

"You want to knock those words back through his teeth while I hold off Craven and Kahn, Edge?" Meyers asked.

The half-breed subdued the impulse to take up the invitation. One man—Wylie—had already died from being in the line of a backlash of anger which should have been directed at another target. And now Edge's subsiding wrath was caused by the unknown sharpshooter, not by Hanson. But while the tall, lean, impassive-faced man pondered this for long seconds Warren Hanson sweated. For Craven and Kahn spoke no word nor made any move to back him and he was again as afraid as during the immediate aftermath of Larry Wylie's death.

"You saw I just washed up, feller," Edge said. "Wouldn't want to get my hands dirty again this soon."

Meyers shrugged and dropped his hand away from his Remington butt. "Suit yourself, mister."

"Usually do," Edge answered. And scratched his right earlobe as he stepped between Hanson on one side and Craven and Kahn on the other.

Then delved the hand into the hair at the nape of his neck, withdrew it and swung what at first looked like a punch toward the side of Warren Hanson's head.

But Meyers knew what it was and yelled, "Don't kill him, Edge!"

This as Craven and Kahn stared in shock and Hanson in horror as they saw the foliage-dappled sunlight-glint on the blade of the straight razor.

Then the honed razor slashed into the flesh of Hanson's right cheek, down from beneath the eye almost to the jawbone, a twist of the wrist and across—not pulled free until the lower stroke of the right angle came close to the ear. Not a deep cut, but bloody one, dark crimson oozing from the lips of the wound to cascade over the flesh and drip to the victim's shirtfront.

"Hot damn, mister!" Kahn gasped.

"You could've poked his eye out!" Craven snarled.

Hanson remained silent as he touched a hand to his face and stared with horrified eyes at the blood on his palm and fingers.

"It was nothing he saw that riled me, feller," Edge told Craven as he wiped the blood off the razor on his own pants before he slid it back into the pouch. "It's the lies he told. For a while, each time he looks in a mirror he'll see the L for liar."

He turned his back on all four men and retraced his path toward the house, as Warren Hanson found his voice and yelled shrilly, "You'll pay for this, you friggin' bastard! Sometime, somehow, I'll make you pay for what you done to me!"

"What the hell?" Kane Worthington snarled as he halted breathless in Edge's path, the scene on the fringe of the timber hidden to him. "What's Hanson whining about, mister?"

The rancher looked angry and worried. Behind him, Ralph Quine scowled his hatred for the half-breed.

"He ain't happy, feller. Guess you could say he just got some bad news."

"He's not the only one," Worthington muttered wearily.

Edge spat at the base of a tree trunk. "Got his in a letter."

CHAPTER EIGHT

EDGE bore down on where the two men stood and they stepped aside, aware from the hard-set face with its glittering slits of eyes that the half-breed's mind was concerned with matters far removed from the incident which had taken place on the other side of the timber.

"Mister, I need to talk to you!" Kane Worthington yelled in his wake.

"Later," came the rasped reply, as Chuck Meyers joined Worthington and Quine. And the raised voices of the rancher and the lawman were soon lost to Edge as he strode resolutely out of the trees, past the cut-under runabout parked on the gravel driveway and around to the courtyard at the rear of the house.

In the forge area of the large stable, the Negro had already shod one of the cowpunchers' horses but both waited while he worked on the second gelding.

"You gonna go after the guy that shot at you?" the shorter of the white men asked as Edge began to saddle his horse in a stall.

"Right, feller."

"Ain't easy, trackin' across Bar-W land," the other cowpuncher warned.

"Easier than sitting around waiting for him to try again."

"Reckon so."

"To my way of thinkin', best not to do nothin' that makes folks want to kill you," the Negro contributed as Edge led the gelding out of the stall and swung up into the saddle.

"Guess that sure is the truth," the short Bar-W hand muttered.

"That's part of his job as a blacksmith," Edge said, noting that May Worthington's stallion was not among the horses in the stalls of the neat stables.

"Tellin' the truth?"

All three were puzzled.

The half-breed hunched his shoulders and leaned forward to ride out of the stable doorway as he growled, "Hitting the nail on the head."

Out in front of the house, the runabout had been moved to the porch. Droplets of drying blood on the whitened step showed that Warren Hanson had been taken into the house. Chuck Meyers had recaptured his horse and was sitting astride it, allowing it to drink from the ornamental pool across which the sharp-shooter had blasted two bullets.

"I meant for you to beat up on him a little is all," the sheriff said harshly, a scowl of contempt on his round face. "I ain't never seen a meaner move than that."

"I ain't got the time to tell you about others," Edge answered.

Meyers' horse had drunk its fill and the lawman tugged on the reins to head the animal toward the gravel driveway. "And I ain't got the time to go huntin' for that sniper, mister. But if I hear you find him and kill him and it ain't in self-defense, I'll come lookin' for you."

In the bright, glaring and hot sunlight of early afternoon the tension which held the narrowed eyes of the two men locked together had an almost palpable presence.

"I ain't in the business of killing, sheriff," the half-breed said after stretched seconds of silence. "Unless the other feller wants to trade that way."

Meyers held the scowl for a moment more, then nodded. "One more thing, mister. Wells Fargo have posted a thousand-dollar reward for the capture of Felipe Cortez. And a hundred dollars each for the five men who were with him when the stage driver and guard were murdered. So if you can get them as well as the Worthington girl, you'll be doin' real good business."

He heeled his horse in one direction as Edge moved the gelding forward in another, the half-breed riding slowly through the trees and out on the far side. Where he dismounted and walked back and forth for a while, until he found sign to show where the sharpshooter had emerged from the timber. Then he remounted and began the slow, painstaking chore of tracking the man who had attempted to kill him.

As he did so, riding across grazing land, through rocky gullies and timber stands, into hollows and around outcrops, splashing along irrigation ditches and just occasionally cresting a rise, he kept his mind clear of any stray thought that was not concerned with tracking the sniper and watching for a sign that the man expected pursuit and was hiding in ambush.

Except once.

When he rode around a hedge-enclosed burial ground and saw a mound of earth on a new grave at the head of which was a temporary wooden marker painted with just today's date and the name Lawrence Wylie. Older graves were marked with marble tombstones with the names and dates expertly chipped out. And as he glanced across the private cemetery, the half-breed reflected briefly upon what May Worthington had told him of her father's ambition to rule the world, wondering cynically if the rancher also ran a midwife service in his valley so that he could take care of Bar-W employees from the womb to the grave.

The cowpuncher had been right. The task Edge had set himself was a difficult one, for the spread supported a great many cows, horses and men to ride herd on the animals, thus the terrain was thick with sign. And all that worked in the half-breed's favor was the fact that the mount of the sharpshooter had thrown the right foreshoe.

Then, after two grueling hours of by turns scouring

the ground and every pocket of cover within rifle range, Edge was able to make more speed. For it became apparent that his quarry, after heading consistently northeastwards along the valley bottom over stock-raising terrain, had then swung to the right a mile or so short of where the farmsteads had been established. To ride out of the valley in a south-eastern direction—taking advantage of the cover of two elongated hillocks that formed a natural, hidden trail on the slope.

At the top of the grade, Edge reined his gelding to a halt and looked half-right down Indian Hill to the town of that name—some two miles distant beyond the scattered farmsteads flanking the two trails that at the foot of the slope became side streets of the community.

From this initial vantage-point, with a blurring haze of heat-shimmer mixed with smoke acting to soften the panoramic view over which he raked his slitted blue eyes, Indian Hill looked a pleasant enough town. But as he rode closer, the harsh reality of what he had seen in the moonlit early hours and at dawn could be witnessed even more clearly under the unremitting glare of the afternoon sun.

And now there was not just Seth Barrow the gravedigger out in the open to show what effect such impoverished surroundings had upon the human condition. For there were men and women engaged in backbreaking work on the arid fields of the farmsteads and a few people moved along the streets of the town, all of them poorly dressed and, whatever their ages, looking old before their time as they shuffled about their business—paying scant attention with dull eyes to the stranger who rode past.

Just as he had done much earlier in the day, Edge hitched his gelding to the rail out front of the Arizona Star and pushed open the batwing doors to enter the saloon.

He left outside the dry heat and smell of decay and relished the pleasant shade and fetid atmosphere filled with the familiar saloon odors of tobacco smoke, liquor and sweat. He was sweating as freely as Chuck Meyers, Seth Barrow and the sour-faced bartender. The bartender was smoking the cheroot and Meyers and the stoop-shouldered old timer were drinking whisky at a table.

The other five tables in the place were vacant, as were most of the shelves along the wall in back of the bar. The sawdust on the floor had not been changed in a long time and the smoke-darkened timber walls of the twenty-by-forty room looked as if no effort had ever been made to clean them.

"He led you to town?" Meyers asked.

"What can I get you?" the bartender wanted to know, disinterestedly.

"Beer. He came out of the valley to the north of town. Figure this is the only place he could have come. Riding a horse with one shoe missing."

He bellied up to the bar, placed some coins on its top, took a swig from the glass set down before him, and turned to look at the lawman.

"He tried for you first, feller. Only took a shot at me after I'd drawn a gun."

Meyers shook his head. "I got no ideas, mister."

"I didn't see a blacksmith's in town."

Barrow aimed for a spittoon, missed and stained the old sawdust still more. "Man that run it was one of them that sold out to Kane Worthington, mister. So the forge was one of the places that Satanas burned down. Next door but one to the church."

Meyers spat, and his aim was better. "Satanas, shit!" he growled. "His name's Cortez, Seth. He ain't nothin' but a drink-pourer turned to crime."

"So where does a man get his horse shod around here?" Edge asked.

"Young feller named Roy Dibble, mister," Barrow answered. "Runs the place highest up on Indian Hill. Found some ready-made shoes in what was left of the forge. Enough to last awhile for the handful of horses we got in town. Just Chuck's here. And Doc Laurie's.

Mr. Benteen's buggy-horse. Few others here and there. Most folks can't run to a horse no more."

"Struggle enough to put feed in our own mouths," the bartender said bitterly.

"The stranger's got troubles of his own, Curtis," the lawman muttered. "And I guess he's seen enough of what's around him to know what ails this town."

"Seems to me," the middle-aged, rat-faced bartender countered, "that he ain't got no troubles here he can't ride away from. A man like him."

"Don't rile him, Curtis," Meyers warned. "He can be real mean when he's riled."

"Like to finish what I start is all," Edge said evenly. "A bad habit of mine."

"But high-payin'," the sheriff pointed out. "You thought any about workin' for the Wells Fargo money as well as what Worthington is payin' you?"

"Kane Worthington won't be paying anybody unless you foot the bill," Cyrus Benteen said as he entered the saloon at the head of a group of five other men.

One of them, like Benteen, was attired in a city-suit, vest and necktie. The other four were in shirtsleeves and wore aprons in the manner of storekeepers. The lawyer's expression matched his grimly serious tone of voice, while the other newcomers were enjoying a sense of satisfaction. All of them were in an early-fifties-to-mid-sixties age-group.

"What the hell's that supposed to mean, Mr. Benteen?" Meyers asked as he got to his feet.

"Explain, Mr. Becker," the lawyer said.

"Isn't this the man—"

While Benteen led the others between the tables to the bar, nodding an acknowledgement when the tender lifted a whisky bottle from a shelf, the other city-suited man remained on the threshold of the saloon, eyeing Edge anxiously. When his gaze was trapped by the blue, glinting slits of the half-breed's eyes, he was frightened into curtailing the question.

The short and fat Benteen realized the reason for

Becker's nervous reticence and nodded in curt greeting when Edge glanced at him.

"This gentleman has as much right to know of Kane Worthington's financial position as anyone else," he said to the room in general. Then, to the half-breed, "Mr. Becker runs the Indian Hill Bank, sir. You may be aware that Mr. Worthington called at the bank this morning."

The sixty-year-old, gray-faced and balding banker was not reassured by the lawyer's explanation. He took out a handkerchief and mopped at his sweat-sheened forehead as he said, "It is most irregular for a man in my position to discuss the business of a client in public."

"Frig that!" a gaunt-faced, bearded storekeeper growled and received grunts of agreement with the view.

"Under normal circumstances, I would entirely concur," Benteen said. "But the present situation is most abnormal."

"This ain't no fancy court hearin'," Meyers put in. "Cut out the five-dollar words and get to the point." He looked hard across the saloon at the sweating banker and asked, "You sayin' Kane Worthington came to you to raise money, Becker?"

The banker sucked in a gulp of air as if he was about to launch into a lengthy reply to the question. Then he sighed the breath from his lungs and nodded as he said, "In short, that is precisely what happened, Sheriff."

"Well, I'll be damned!" the bartender rasped.

And Seth Barrow spat, scored a hit in the spittoon and thumped a fist gleefully on the table top.

"If that's the short of it, feller," Edge said evenly, "what's the long?"

Meyers nodded that he wanted to know this, too.

"I'd rather you explained, Cyrus," Becker blurted. "It was bad enough telling you people."

With this, he turned and retreated hurriedly from the Arizona Star.

"Damned old woman," the bartender snorted, and then grinned as the storekeepers signaled for another round of drinks.

"You then," Edge said, pointing a brown-skinned finger at Benteen, recalling the constant anxiety which he had seen on Kane Worthington's face—that had receded only during the time he was frantically beating up on his daughter. An emotion which had been at odds with the image of a man of wealth and power who looked upon the world as his oyster.

"Very well. Kane Worthington is over-extended. Not in the day-to-day running of his affairs, I should add. But he does not have sufficient liquid assets to meet the considerable extra expense necessary to secure the safe return of his daugheter, Grace."

"You mean the sonofabitch is broke, mister?" Seth Barrow asked. "Is that what he means, Chuck?"

"No, he don't mean that," Meyers snapped impatiently. "He means that Kane Worthington can't just open a safe at the ranch and take out fifty thousand greenbacks."

"Fifty-two thousand is the amount that's needed," Edge said evenly. "How much can he raise?"

"Really, I must support Mr. Becker's view as far as inquiries of that nature are concerned," Cyrus Benteen complained. "There is no need to air every last detail of Mr. Worthington's financial affairs. The important question is: are enough people in this town prepared to loan the necessary funds to him."

"Loan him?" Meyers exclaimed.

"We said somethin' like that Chuck," the bearded storekeeper growled, and vented a hollow laugh.

"Only not so polite," a man with a crooked nose amplified.

Benteen scowled at the storekeepers, blatantly despising them. "There may be others in this town not prepared to use the life or death of a young woman as a bargaining tool."

The bearded man snorted. "And someplace there may be pigs with wings, mister!"

"Cut out the cross-talk and get to the friggin' point!" Meyers snarled.

"Sure, Chuck," a soft-spoken, innocuous-looking man with a pencil-thin moustache offered. His features setting into a grin of evil delight as he continued, "Way we figure it, only way Kane Worthington is gonna get money out of us is if he sells us pieces of the Bar-W."

There were long seconds of silence in the hot shade of the saloon. Then the lawman showed a grin which became a chuckle, the bartender threw back his head and laughed to the smoke-blackened ceiling. And Seth Barrow broke out into a childish giggle. The four storekeepers joined in the mirth. While Cyrus Benteen looked like he was going to be sick. And Edge drank the remainder of his beer and set the glass back on the bartop.

Meyers, grinning again, drew a dollar from his hip pocket and waved it at the bartender. "A beer for everyone, Curtis. We got cause for celebratin'."

"Count me out, feller," Edge said, pushing away from the bar as the sounds of triumphant laughter subsided.

"Me, too," Benteen rasped through teeth clenched in tightly controlled anger.

"No need for you to go runnin' off to tell Worthington the bad news, stranger," the bearded storekeeper called harshly. "He's due in town any time now to hear it himself from us."

At the open batwings, Edge stopped and looked back over his shoulder as the fat little lawyer brushed angrily past him. "If you see me running anyplace," he drawled, "I'll be trying to catch up with the feller I'm chasing."

Outside on the sun-bright street between the dilapidated buildings and the fire-ravaged ruins of those put to the torch, Cyrus Benteen was leaning against the water trough beside the Arizona Star hitching rail. He was taking deep breaths of the hot air, the freshness of which was marred only by the smell of decay which clung to Indian Hill.

"In a way, you can't blame them," he said dully as he stared across the street to the bank, where Becker could be seen, sitting morosely behind a desk. "When they didn't do what Kane Worthington wanted, he set out to ruin them."

Edge swung up into the saddle and glanced bleakly along the street in each direction. "Looks like he's not doing too bad a job. Last town I'd come to if I aimed to raise fifty-two thousand dollars."

"Ten thousand is what he needs, Mr. Edge. And there is ample on deposit at Becker's bank to cover it. Indian Hill used to be a prosperous town, I understand. Not since I've been here, though. Which is not long. I work for a legal office in Tucson which handles Mr. Worthington's business affairs. But when so many property deals started to go through, it was better for me to come to Indian Hill temporarily."

He sighed. "But that is by the by. The fact is that many of the town's merchants were thrifty during the good times. And the bank has a reserve, of course. And there are sufficient funds available to cover the difference between the cash money which Mr. Worthington has to hand and the sum to secure Miss Worthington's safe release."

Edge had been rolling a cigarette while Benteen talked. Now he struck a match on the stock of his booted Winchester and asked through a stream of tobacco smoke, "How much will the ten grand cost him?"

The lawyer's round, fleshy face showed a grimace. "The Bar-W property is worth at least a hundred dollars an acre. The four men in the saloon—and they will have no trouble in gaining the agreement of others—plan to offer fifty cents. Which will secure them the entire valley for ten thousand dollars. In criminal law, which is not my field, such a deal comes close to being tantamount to exortion."

Edge eased his gelding back from the hitching rail and turned him. "Law books got a name for what Kane Worthington did to this town, feller?" he asked evenly.

Benteen got the sick look on his face again. "I said that in a way, they could not be blamed. But in their vindictiveness, they have chosen to ignore the fact that an innocent young woman could well be murdered. Amelia and I rode the stage from Tucson with Miss Grace and it emerged from our conversations that the young lady is adamantly opposed to her father's methods. I made this clear during the meeting at the bank. But was shouted down."

"She say why she went to Tucson?" Edge asked.

"To visit the grave of her mother," Benteen replied, obviously puzzled by the half-breed's reason for the question. "Gertrude Worthington died at their home there just before the house in the valley was ready for occupation. Grace goes there once a month to place flowers on the grave." Suddenly, he nodded. "Yes, I see why you asked, sir. The trips were common knowledge, so the Mexican knew which stage Grace would be on."

"Obliged," Edge said absently as he heeled his horse along the street and then steered him to the left, was soon back on the narrow trail that snaked up the hillside between the farmsteads.

In the fields that were still being worked, the men and women did not glance up at him this time. There was no one hoeing the weeds from the stony and dusty soil of the three acres surrounding the small adobe house and the larger frame barn that comprised the Dibble place. But smoke was curling lazily from a stone chimney that was built against an end wall of the house. And a smell of cooking penetrated out from the cracks around the door and the shutters which were closed upon the single window, an aroma that caused the half-breed's stomach to rumble its emptiness as he rode slowly through a gap in the barbed-wire fence that marked the boundary of Roy Dibble's property.

"What you want?" a man demanded, the harshly voiced question shouted through the center crack in the ill-fitting window shutters.

"Looking for a horse," Edge answered as he reined in his gelding on the hard-packed dirt of the yard out front of the house. "Which I could maybe eat since the owner won't have no more use for it."

"There ain't no horse here! And you can eat in town! Turn around and get off my place!"

In the barn, a horse whinnied.

"You're a liar, Dibble," the half-breed drawled, and arced the butt of his cigarette away. "Got that straight from the horse's mouth."

"Beat it!" There was a note of panic underlying the man's anger now. "If you don't, I'll blast you! I got the right! You being on my property!"

It was the fear which had taken a hold on Roy Dibble that caused Edge to comply with the order. For somebody as scared as he was could likely carry out the threat without pause for thought. And, totally exposed in the center of the yard, the half-breed had not the slightest chance of surviving a fusillade of shots.

"I'll call again," he said as he tugged on the reins to turn the horse.

"You'll get the same thing then!" Dibble called after him as he rode out through the gap in the fence. And made a right turn to head off the end of the trail, veered right again and then reined in his mount as soon as he was out of sight from the front of the small house.

He slid from the saddle and took the Winchester from the boot as part of the same move. He paused a few seconds to ease his topcoat off the bedroll and then, with long strides, went silently toward the rear of the adobe house. The roof had a low pitch with the slope from the front to the back. There was a wooden trough along the length of the rear wall to catch infrequent rainwater and by using this he was able to get up onto the roof without difficulty.

88

He could hear no sounds from beneath him and made none of his own as he bellied along a diagonal line across the roof.

On other farmsteads further down Indian Hill, men and women continued with their chores, unaware of the half-breed on the roof of the Dibble house. Only smoke from an occasional chimney showed that the community at the foot of the slope was not yet a ghost town.

A few moments later, the chimney of the Dibble house no longer gave off smoke as it was blocked by the half-breed's coat—screwed up into a ball and jammed into the aperture. And he was down on his belly again, inching to the front lip of the roof. Where he waited, rifle aimed down into the yard, finger to the trigger and hand positioned to pump the lever action of the Winchester.

The sun beating down out of the sky of scattered high cloud penetrated the fabric of his shirt and pants to burn his back and legs. Time seemed to slow down, but Edge had always been a patient man.

Roy Dibble coughed. Then cursed. But the thick solidness of the roof acted to muffle the sounds.

The shriller tones of a woman's voice made for more clarity when she snapped, "What's wrong with the damn stove?"

Then came the frantic scrape of metal against metal as the man worked the damper.

"Open the door and shutter, will you!" he snarled.

Bolts were drawn from brackets and timber slammed against walls—the shutters to the outside and the door to the in. Smoke wisped and then billowed out into the bright sunlight, the strong smell of wood masking the appetizing aroma of cooking food.

Edge jacked a shell into the breech of the rifle, his face impassive.

"It's no damn good! We gotta get outside!"

The woman emerged first, at a run. And Edge received a fleeting impression through the thickening smoke of a tall, thin woman dressed in pants and shirt. Then Dibble appeared. He had a bare torso. Both of them were coughing.

Edge stood up, side-stepped to the chimney, jerked his coat free and draped it over one shoulder as he returned to the front of the roof.

The couple continued to be wracked by choking coughs as the smoke began to thin, bent over double and clutching their throats. The woman was May Worthington. Roy Dibble did not wear a gunbelt.

The half-breed exploded two fast shots and the bullets kicked up divots of the hard, packed dirt of the yard—one between each pair of splayed feet.

Further down the hill, the field workers snapped their heads around to stare fearfully up at the source of the rifle shots. But none was so fast in reflex action as the Worthington woman and Dibble, who whirled, straightened, threw back their heads and held their breath as they raked their eyes toward Edge.

Then the half-breed pumped the action of the Winchester again, as Dibble recovered from the shock and shifted his gaze from the roof to the open doorway of the house.

"If I have to labor the point again, feller," Edge drawled, "you could get bored to death."

"Point?" May Worthington croaked.

He allowed the rifle to dip down until its barrel end rested against the lip of the roof above the open doorway. "That there ain't no smoke without fire."

He squeezed the trigger.

CHAPTER NINE

ROY Dibble was close to thirty years of age. He was not tall, but he had a powerful build. He had light brown hair, almost blond, and a handsome face composed of regular features—the kind of face that would become more goodlooking with maturity. Toiling long hours on the arid soil of Indian Hill had toughened and darkened his skin but his light blue eyes were clear and bright, as if there had been little mental anxiety accompanying the hard physical labor of his chosen way of life.

"I ain't no good at word games, mister!" he said while May continued to shake from the effect of seeing the third bullet bury itself in the dirt of the house threshold.

Thus as Edge dropped to his haunches, rested a hand on the lip of the roof and jumped to the ground. He landed sure-footed and well-balanced. "Gunsport more in your line, feller?"

"What is that supposed to mean, Edge?" May Worthington asked, and needed a great effort to keep a tremor from her voice.

"Your stallion in the barn, lady?"

On the hill, the homesteaders had returned to their work. Nobody had moved out of town to check on the reason for the shots.

"Yes. Why?"

"We don't have to tell him anythin', May," Dibble snarled.

"You want to bet on that?" Edge rasped. "A bullet

91

to a hole where it'll take a long time for your life to run out through."

"He doesn't make idle threats, Roy," the woman warned, regaining her composure by the moment. "What about my horse, Edge?"

"Like for you to bring him out here."

"What for?"

"Want to see if he's thrown the right foreshoe."

Dibble's defiant attitude was suddenly displaced by a renewal of panic, but he had no gun in his hand this time. While the woman showed the extent to which she had recovered by replying evenly, "The shoe is missing sure enough. He threw it while I was riding out here to Roy's earlier. Why on earth should that be of the least concern to you?"

"Good try, lady," Edge countered, and backed in through the doorway. "But your playmate ain't any good at lying games, either."

The hot interior of the house still smelled heavily of smoke. The half-breed saw a Winchester leaning against the wall beside the window and rested his own on a table while he pumped the action of Dibble's rifle. And was able to watch the couple outside as he counted the unspent shells that were ejected and spun to the dirt floor.

Dibble kept clenching and opening his fists at his sides while May Worthington worked hard at keeping her poise from cracking. Soon, the rifle was empty.

"Two short of a full load," Edge said flatly. "Two shots. Two misses, Dibble. Is there anything you're good at?"

"We gotta tell him, May," the frightened man blurted. And raised one clenched fist to his mouth and began to chew on the fleshy part of the forefinger. "If he was out at Felipe's place like he says, he probably knows some of it anyway."

"You fool, Roy!" the woman snarled. "A man like him can't be trusted! He only does anything for

92

money! And he's in the pocket of the richest man in the territory! It'll ruin everything."

Edge exchanged his own rifle for the empty Winchester and raked his narrowed eyes over the crudely furnished, single room of the house. There was the stove at one end with a narrow single bed at the other. The table with a chair each side of it in the center. Against the rear wall was a row of wooden boxes and cardboard cartons, most empty and a few stocked with meager supplies of canned foods, crockery, cooking and eating utensils. And there was a trunk under the bed.

"Beans smell good," the half-breed said, beckoning with his free hand for the couple to come back inside the house. "Why don't we all eat a hearty meal? In case it turns out to be the last for one of us?"

Dibble came inside first, as Edge sat at the table, facing the door and window, and leaned the rifle against his chair. The man was still afraid. May Worthington, sharing her anger equally between Dibble and the half-breed, trailed the homesteader.

"It was her idea, mister. It took a lot for her to make me do what I done. I ain't no killer."

"That's just because you're such a lousy shot, feller." Edge waved him to the chair across the table, and as soon as Dibble was seated he drew the Colt. "Ask you to take a seat too, lady," he went on. "But after what your pa did to you, I guess I wouldn't be doing you any favor. So you bring me some beans. Then you can stand easy."

He rested the base of the Colt butt on the table, muzzle aimed at Dibble's diaphragm, and cocked the hammer.

Dibble swallowed hard and fastened a tight, frightened grip to each side of his chair seat.

May's plain face colored with an expanding anger and she seemed to take firm root in the doorway of the squalid house. "I wouldn't bring you a cup of water if you were dying of thirst, Edge!" she answered, speaking quietly but coating each word with venom.

Edge sighed and rotated the gun a little so that it was leveled at her thin frame. "He's already made it plain that he wants to talk, lady. So I don't need you for anything I can do myself. Maybe I'll see you in Hell. Goodbye."

"No!" Dibble shrieked. And threw himself sideways out of the chair, was unbalanced for a fraction of a second then stood solidly in the line of fire. He stared for another moment into the glittering slits of Edge's eyes, then screwed his head around to stare at the woman. "You said it yourself. He doesn't make idle threats. Do like he says. Please!"

For a whole stretched second the woman's defiance hardened. But then the rigidity went out of her stance. "Very well, Roy," she said wearily and advanced on the stove. "But it's likely he'll kill us both anyway."

Relief had an exhausting effect on Dibble and he almost collapsed back on to the chair. The muzzle of the Colt tracked him.

"Tell it, feller."

Dibble was breathing heavily and there was a croak in his voice when he replied. "You have to know it all if it's gonna make any sense, mister."

The woman banged onto the table a plate piled high with beans and stabbed a spoon into the center of the food.

"They say interesting conversation aids the digestion," Edge drawled as he transferred the revolver to his left hand and pulled the plate in front of him.

Dibble watched May Worthington go to the doorway where she took up a position with her back to the room: and stared fixedly down the slope of Indian Hill at the town. Then the bare-chested man got a fixed stare of his own into his light blue eyes, which became locked onto the dark hole of the Colt muzzle.

"Grace and me, we're in love," he opened. "Been that way for a long time. Ever since we rode the stage back from Tucson together. But it had to be in secret on account of her father being the way he is. Only times we ever got to see each other was when she could sneak up outta the valley. Dead of the night mostly. She'd come up over the hill from the north, the way you trailed her sister today."

"Isn't it a romantic tale, Edge?" May put in sourly.

Dibble's temper flared. "Don't you put us down, you bitch!" he snarled, but he did not turn his head to look at her.

"Sure is, lady," the half-breed allowed evenly after swallowing a mouthful of beans. "And if you interrupt again it could turn out to have a real heart-stopping moment."

May cursed softly.

"Kane Worthington is the hardest and meanest son-ofabitch I ever did see," Dibble went on after a moment of relishing Edge's uncompromising rebuke of the woman. "I guess you know what he did to Indian Hill?"

"Yeah."

"And about how Felipe Cortez hit town and burned down every damn property Worthington had bought?"

"Yeah."

For a moment, Dibble seemed disappointed that he was to be denied the opportunity of telling the whole story of Worthington's empire building ambition and its frustrations. Then he sighed. "And I reckon you know that Grace ain't exactly a prisoner of Felipe and his men?"

Edge chewed beans and did not even respond by altering the impassive set of his features. And his silence spread anxiety across the handsome face of Dibble as May turned from the waist to direct a quizzical look at the half-breed. The tacit question remained in her eyes for perhaps two seconds. Then an evil smile became pasted to her unbeautiful face.

"You can kill me if you like, Edge," she invited. "I'll die happy now."

Her harsh laugh triggered Dibble into a fast, enraged move, as clumsy as when he had earlier lunged to protect her from the dispassionate half-breed. But this time it was he who meant her harm.

The Colt exploded a shot, the sound of the report very loud within the confines of the room and the acrid taint of burnt powder was pungent—masking the stale smell of old smoke that previously permeated the hot air.

Dibble screamed and was flung back down into his chair by the impact of the bullet tearing into his elbow from the inside of the joint. From the range of a table's width, the shell shattered bone and burst clear at the rear of the man's arm amid a spray of blood droplets and displaced tissue.

The eruption of violence did not alter one line of the smile on May Worthington's face. While Dibble's features were drained of color by pain and shock as he clutched at the wound in his right arm with his left hand. And stared at the bean-chewing Edge like a whipped dog who does not know the reason for the beating.

Edge rattled his spoon down on the empty plate and slid the Colt into its holster. "Owed you for trying to kill me, feller. I'm ready to call us even on that. If I have to send you to the big farm in the sky now, it'll be on account of something else you do. Or don't do." He took out the makings and began to roll a cigarette. "Right now, all I want from you are words."

"Go to hell, you hard bastard! Or backshoot me to send me there! I'm going to see Cortez!"

He got to his feet and the chair tipped over backwards. He swayed and swallowed hard, grimacing as if it was acrid tasting bile that had risen to his throat. He was still holding on to the wounded elbow. But then both his arms flopped to his sides and, as he made to turn toward the doorway, the delayed reaction to the assault on his nervous system hit him.

"Oh, my God," he rasped as he felt the strength drain out of him. And then he collapsed into unconsciousness. His limp body slammed hard to the dirt floor.

Edge struck a match on the table top and lit his cigarette.

"The fools!" May snarled as her grin became a sneer. "Trusting the Mexican. After he murdered those men on the stage, it was obvious to me Cortez had no intention of helping anybody but himself. But not Dibble, he still thought—"

"Your father keeps you and your sister on a short rein is how it looks," Edge cut in. "And she and the farmer here want to live happy ever after in some roses around the door cottage a long way from the Bar-W. But they need a stake to set themselves up and for a share of the action Cortez said he'd help. How do you fit into that, lady? And why were you so anxious to have him kill me and the local lawman?"

Bitterness now had a firm hold on the woman's thin features and she nodded several times while the half-breed spoke. Then,

"Tight rein is right, Edge. To father, Grace and I are as much possessions as his cows and horses and his house and land. So much so that it's surprising he never burned the Bar-W brand into our hides. We're both grown women and yet he treats us like children. The only allowance he makes is that we're both ready for marriage. For me, it's past time for that.

"But he picks likely candidates for husbands. Or he used to, until Grace and I had spit in the eye of every rich man's son he invited to the house. To put us on show like goods he had to trade." The harshness went out of her tone and expression and something akin to self-pity replaced it. "I guess he never had much hope for me—with the kind of looks I have. Which is why he didn't give a damn when he found out the reason for my early morning rides around the valley. So long as I was only making myself available to Bar-W men— bought and paid for and owned by him—he thought it was all right. Not good, but all right. At least I wasn't asking anything from him. Especially money."

"Then your sister figured out a way of taking him for a big bundle, lady?"

A curt nod. "Yes, she did. The sneaky little bitch! Without telling me anything about it. There never was ever any love lost between us. Mainly because of Grace being younger and prettier than me, Father always had higher hopes of her bringing more money and property into the family, and she was always his favorite. And Grace sucked up to him. Always had a good excuse for not taking to any of the suitors he picked for her. Used to tell him how much she appreciated what he was trying to do for her. And give him wheedling apologies when it never ever worked out."

"I'd like for the beans to stay in my belly, lady."

"What?" She was jerked out of an embittered reverie on the jealousy-ridden past.

"I'm getting a little sick of listening to your family problems," Edge augmented.

"All right, damn you!" She stamped her foot. "I'll cut it short for you. I found out about Grace's secret trips out here to see this clod of a dirtfarmer. Saw her sneaking back home early one morning. So I started to watch her and I followed her to this hovel. I listened outside and heard them talking about the plan for her to be kidnapped by Felipe Cortez. How father would pay the ransom and how they would give a share to the Mexican and use the rest to get away from here and get married.

"At first I was going to warn father. But then I realized that would be acting like the spiteful small child he seems to think I am. And he wouldn't have thanked me for it. Kane Worthington never appreciates anything anyone does for him. So I bided my time, waiting for an opportunity whereby I could get a share of the money."

From his chair at the table, Edge was able to look out through the window and down the slope of Indian

Hill to the town. Except for the gaps in the building line where Worthington property had been burned, little of the street was visible. But a stretch of the west trail was and he could see riders advancing along it. Seven men on horseback, trailing Kane Worthington's cut-under runabout.

"I don't have much more time to waste, lady," he told the thin woman in the doorway.

"Grace may not have much more time to live, mister," she countered. "Which doesn't concern me overmuch except that dead she's not worth fifty cents, let alone fifty thousand dollars. And after Father had beaten me this morning in such humiliating circumstances, I was more determined than ever to make him pay and to get my fair share of the money.

"So I rode out here to talk with Roy Dibble. And I did some straight talking to the crazy fool. I told him I knew all about the plan and he started to shake like a leaf when I warned him I'd tell father if he didn't do exactly as I told him."

"Kill me before I decided to tell your father Grace was a party to her own kidnapping?"

A flicker of fear showed in the woman's pale green eyes, but she regained control very quickly. "That's right. And he agreed fast when I pointed out that Father wouldn't care two hoots what happened to Grace if he discovered the truth. And that Felipe Cortez wouldn't hesitate to kill her if he didn't get the money he demanded.

"Dibble used to be a good customer of the cantina in the old days and at first the crazy fool wouldn't hear a word against the Mexican. Until I reminded him how Cortez murdered those two Wells Fargo men for doing absolutely nothing."

"And you waited here and sweated while Dibble rode your horse to the house to do some murdering of his own?"

Her fear took longer to be subdued this time as the

soft-spoken words penetrated her mind and she stared at the impassive profile of the half-breed who continued to watch the men down on the trail.

"Yes. Sweating and thinking—that with you out of the way, there was only me, Dibble, Grace and Cortez and his men who knew about the trickery. And none of us was likely to warn Father."

The man on the floor groaned and his legs and good arm twitched. And May Worthington scowled down at him as she added,

"But the stupid fool failed. He claims he's a fine shot, but that when he saw you with Sheriff Meyers, he went haywire."

"Obliged," Edge said, and belched as he rose from the chair, picking up the rifle.

The woman backed out of the doorway ahead of him as he advanced on her. "Is . . . is that all?" she asked, her hands and voice trembling.

"What else is there?" he countered, adjusting the smoke-smelling coat over his shoulder.

"You . . . you shot Roy Dibble for trying to kill you. I've admitted I told him to do it."

Edge nodded and looked at her now that Kane Worthington and his men had ridden onto the main street of Indian Hill and were hidden from view by the buildings. "If you were anybody else, lady, I'd likely kill you for that," he drawled. "But since you are who you are, I figure life is going to be worse than death for you."

"You bastard!" she snarled.

"You were fathered by one of that kind by all accounts."

He went to the side of the house and saw that the gelding had wandered just a few feet from where he had left him. When he pursed his lips and vented a low whistle, the horse raised his head, whinnied and came toward him.

"You think I'm going back to the Bar-W and Kane Worthington if you give me any choice?"

"You've got the choice, lady," Edge told her as he

100

slid the Winchester in the boot and swung into the saddle. "But then you always have, seems to me." He waved a hand to left and right. "Big, wide, hard world out there, though. Where black stallions and soft beds in clean rooms cost money that ain't easy to come by. Where there are more places like Dibble's dirt farm than there are like the Bar-W spread. And where even fine-looking women can't get a man to screw them at the drop of a chemise—and then get them to quiet at the drop of a rich father's name." He touched the brim of his hat and added, "Luck to you."

"You bastard!" she repeated, but this time rasped it through teeth clenched in a snarl.

This as Roy Dibble, a grimace of pain on his handsome face, staggered into the doorway and sagged against the frame.

"What's happenin'?" he asked, blinking against the glare of the late afternoon sun.

"What does it look like, you crazy fool?" May Worthington flung at the suffering and uncomprehending man. "He got what he came for and now he's leaving."

"Is that right?" Dibble asked, and relief to be rid of the glinting eyed half-breed so lightly started to show on his pale face.

"Sure is," Edge answered and glanced coldly at the scowling woman and the still-puzzled man before he heeled his horse out of the yard. "Plain and simple."

CHAPTER TEN

EDGE was aware of watching eyes as he rode in off the trail and started along the side street.

From further away, Chuck Meyers shouted. "Don't try it."

The half-breed reined in his horse on the center of the narrow street between two derelict houses with broken windows and sagging stoops.

"Kill anyone who gets in your way!" Kane Worthington roared.

And a rifle shot resounded back and forth from the façades of the buildings flanking Indian Hill's main street.

Edge knew he was being watched from behind a cracked, grime-encrusted window to the left of the doorway of the house on his right. He did not look in that direction as he slid the Winchester from the boot and eased out of the saddle, by swinging a leg up and over the gelding's neck and dropping to the ground.

"Mr. Worthington said for you to keep out of this, Edge," the man said, his voice hard, as he stepped forward to show himself at the window.

He was another of the rancher's hard-eyed deputies, standing with his thumbs hooked over his belt buckle.

"That's just a warning, Meyers!" Kane Worthington snarled. "If I have to fire again, it won't be high."

"All the tickets been sold, feller?" Edge asked, canting the rifle to his shoulder.

"What?"

"Like to see the gunplay," the half-breed answered

and started forward, turning his back on the man at the window.

He glanced back over his shoulder when the door of the abandoned house creaked open and footfalls hit the hard-packed ground outside.

"I got my orders, mister!" the tall, broad-shouldered, narrow-waisted, red-haired man of about thirty snarled. And draped a hand over his holstered Colt.

"All right, Ralph!" Worthington shouted. "Go bring out what we came for."

"You hitting the bank, feller?" Edge asked.

"Yeah," the deputy answered, made nervous by indecision.

A nod as the half-breed faced front again. "Your boss has a reputation for getting what he wants. Come noon tomorrow, he'll need me more than you. If you pull that gun, use it."

He started forward and felt an itch between his shoulder blades. But knew it was caused by the man's eyes, rather than his gun-muzzle, leveled at the spot.

"Hell, mister, you sure make life difficult for people!" the deputy snarled, and took long strides to catch up with the half-breed.

"Into every life a little rain must fall, feller."

"It ain't stopped pourin' down since you showed up here," the man growled.

Edge spat ahead of him and the arid surface of the street soaked up the saliva before his boot stepped on the spot. "Only on folks who ain't got the sense to get in out of the wet, feller."

He and the deputy swung around the corner and surveyed the western stretch on the town's main street which had been shrouded in silence since the rancher had shouted the last order to Ralph Quine.

Now Worthington's top deputy was in process of doing what his boss had commanded. He was midway across the street between the Arizona Star and the Indian Hill bank, a half-pace ahead of six other men. All of them with handguns drawn and leveled and with tin

104

stars pinned to their shirts, the shiny metal glinting in the rays of the sinking sun that cast the men's shadows long and narrow on the street. Hanson, with a white dressing on his right cheek, Kahn and Craven were in the advancing line. Which was faced by Chuck Meyers who was flanked by Becker and Cyrus Benteen, this trio aligned in front of the bank's open doorway. The sheriff had a Winchester sloped across the front of his body while the banker and the lawyer were unarmed.

Worthington's runabout was parked at the side of the street just short of the bank, but the powerfully built, gray-haired rancher was not aboard. He stood on the stoop of the saloon, just outside the fastened-open batwing doors. A Winchester was aimed from his shoulder, to draw a bead on Sheriff Meyers through a gap in the line of slow-moving deputies.

There was no one else on the street, but the tension in the watching eyes of witnesses concealed in nearby buildings seemed to create a palpable presence in the cooling air and failing light of afternoon-meeting-evening. While on the strip of street between the saloon and the bank, fear hovered like an invisible yet tangible cloud of poisonous vapor.

"Hold it there!" the moustached sheriff barked.

And the deputies complied in unison. The halting of their slow advance signaled a second of total silence, curtailed by the footfalls of Edge and the man at his side. Which drew every pair of eyes toward them.

"I gave you an order, Tuttle!" Kane Worthington roared.

Edge sensed a sidelong, pleading glance from the man at his side. Called, "He passed it on, feller! We neither of us figured it was worth dying for!"

"Edge, they plan to rob the bank!" Cyrus Benteen shouted.

"He's with Worthington!" Chuck Meyers snarled at the frightened lawyer.

"Wrong, I'm with me," the half-breed countered as he and Tuttle continued along the street, both of them

105

cracking their eyes against the fading glare of the setting sun. "Until somebody comes up with some money."

"Don't interfere in this and you'll get paid," Worthington assured coldly as he switched his concentrated attention back to Meyers. "You know what the people of this town want of me?"

"I heard," Edge answered as he and Tuttle came to a halt on the sidelines of the stand-off.

But the scowling, rigidly erect rancher continued as if there had been no response to his rhetorical query. "My daughter is in mortal danger and their price for her safety is me giving up the Bar-W. For frigging chicken-feed." The Winchester wavered as Worthington's rising anger caused his hands to tremble. "Can you believe that?" he snarled. "This bunch of hay-seeds trying to screw me? Kane Worthington!"

"It's the depositors' money and their decision, sir," the gray-faced and balding Becker said, needing to gulp down his fear after every two words. "By the rules of the bank, I must abide by it."

"Screw the frigging rules!" Worthington raged. "Quine, go do as I told you!"

"I said to hold it!" Meyers roared, louder and deeper than the rancher: and the knuckles of his fists showed white as he tightened his grip on the rifle. His words and the undeniable resolution in his stance and expression caused the line of deputies to remain where they were. Just Quine shot a glance over his shoulder to look at Worthington—and as his eyes momentarily swept across the face of Edge, they expressed a depthless hatred. "I don't have a cent in the bank," Meyers went on. "What I do have is a tin star on my chest. And that means I have to uphold the law. Bank robbery's against the law, Mr. Worthington."

"So is something called extortion, Meyers!" the rancher countered, less heatedly but offering no compromise in the way he maintained the aim of the rifle.

"Which is the crime the carpetbagging bastards of this town tried against me."

"Ain't no worse than what you did to Indian Hill, Worthington!" Seth Barrow jeered from inside the saloon.

"Keep out of this, old timer!" Meyers yelled, and glanced to his left and right. "You too, Mr. Becker, Mr. Benteen. This is law business."

He gestured with the rifle and Becker scurried away immediately, looking weak with relief. That fat little lawyer hesitated, licking his lips. But then his wife pleaded tearfully, "Do as the sheriff tells you, Cyrus! He's told you to come away. There's no shame in it."

This decided him and he moved quickly out of the line of fire from the deputies' guns, then forced himself to slow and continued at a dignified walk into the town's single office building.

"Don't try to be a hero, Meyers," Worthington urged and now there was a pleading tone underlying his words. "I didn't bring my men here to rob the bank. All I need is a loan. And everyone knows why I need it. I came here earlier today to request the loan—businessman to banker. Offered to repay it at double the base interest rate within a week at the latest. I was refused and—"

"You weren't refused, sir!" Becker corrected shrilly from the hardware store where he had taken refuge. "I told you I would have to put the proposition to my depositors."

The interruption stoked Worthington's anger anew. "I know your friggin' depositors and what they think of me, sir! So I knew what their decision would be! And I've brought my men here to overrule that decision! Kindly stand aside, sheriff. I am a duly appointed marshal of the Territory of Arizona and my men are sworn-in deputies! We are here to confiscate bank money which will be used to save the life of an innocent woman! When that purpose has been accomplished,

107

the money will be returned! And I'm damned if I'll even pay minimum interest! Talk's finished!"

He nodded curtly to Quine, who spoke a soft word and started across the street again. The other deputies in the line were just a beat later in recommencing the advance on the lone figure of Chuck Meyers.

The Indian Hill lawman made to swing his rifle down. The fear of certain death showed in his eyes and his lips beneath the thick moustache moved to form a word that might have been voiced as a curse or a plea or an acknowledgement of defeat.

All eyes were upon him or the men facing him. Until a bullet blasted from the barrel of the half-breed's Winchester. There had been movement and sounds before this—as Edge whipped the rifle down from his shoulder, thumbed back the hammer and rasped,

"Crazy sonofabitch!"

The bullet took Meyers in the right shoulder, forced him into a half-turn and slammed him sideways into the front wall of the bank. His Winchester slipped from his hands and bounced off his boots to the ground.

Another moment of intense silence blanketed Indian Hill, as the shadows of twilight crowded in and the redness in the western sky shaded darker.

Then Ralph Quine snarled, "Come on!" and lunged into a run—reached Meyers in time to snatch the revolver from his holster before the sheriff could touch it with his left hand.

Craven was hard on his heels and used a boot to kick open the bank door. Then the other deputies reached their objective—and Quine was able to delegate the chore of watching Meyers to a scowling Warren Hanson while he entered the bank.

Attention, which had switched from Edge to the storming of the bank, now returned to the tall, lean half-breed as he pumped the action of the Winchester to eject the spent shellcase and then sloped the rifle to his shoulder again. The most powerful stare was directed from the inky black, narrowed-to-slits eyes of

Chuck Meyers as the man leaned his back against the bank wall and slid down on to his haunches, clawed left hand clutching at the bloody wound in his right shoulder.

"You must really be hungry for that two grand, mister," he rasped through gritted teeth. "But you should've killed me."

"Doctor Laurie, get out here and attend to the sheriff!" Kane Worthington roared. And lowered the rifle to a one-handed grip at his side as he stepped down from the saloon stoop. "And be grateful to Edge, Meyers. I was within a half-second of firing. And I would have killed you, make no mistake."

He beckoned for Tuttle to join him and both of them stepped between the half-breed and the sheriff to enter the bank.

"If I was dead, you might have got away with it, mister," Meyers went on, after sparing a brief glance of deep hatred for the rancher. "Because there ain't anyone with any spunk around here gives a damn about me—"

"Seems to me you don't give much of a damn about yourself, feller," Edge drawled as a tall, elderly man with stooped shoulders emerged from the office building and crossed the street. And lights showed here and there at windows to keep the full dark of night away.

Meyers moved his blood-run hand away from the shoulder wound to stab a thumb backwards at his badge of office. "I don't wear this for decoration, mister. And it sure ain't for the money I get paid. Law's the law and you just broke it. More ways than I'm gonna trouble to count right now."

"Noble son of a gun, isn't he?" the lanky Indian Hill doctor growled in a Scottish-accented voice as he reached the front of the bank and gazed down at the injured lawman.

Hanson muttered, "I guess he won't be causin' no more trouble, Doc?"

"Only as a patient, my boy," Laurie answered.

109

"Yeah, go in and join the other toy deputies," Meyers growled. "Be a while before I'm able to make you or anyone else answer for what's happened here today."

"Aye, a real noble gentleman born too late and in the wrong country," the doctor went on after the scowling Hanson had gone into the bank. "He should have been born a few centuries ago in my native country. When I am sure he would have ridden a white charger and carried a sword and a lance with which he could have righted wrongs and rescued fair damsels in every kind of distress."

Meyers grimaced and grunted as he used the wall to help him to his feet, but shook off the helping hand which Laurie extended.

"Quit that crap and start patchin' me up, Doc," he snarled. "I got work to do!"

Laurie sighed. "Doubtless making more work for me."

The lawman jerked a thumb in through the bank doorway and fixed his stare to the impassive face of Edge. "Armed bank robbery's a capital offense in this county. You'll only be needed to attend the executions and pronounce these men dead, Doc."

"Aye, you would have made a fine knight in shining armor, Chuck," Laurie said in the same light tone he had used from the start. "What do you say, sir?"

Only as Laurie turned toward him at close quarters did Edge smell the scent of whisky on the man's breath. And see the network of tiny blood vessels crisscrossing the whites of his eyes.

"Not much, usually."

"Ah, the mark of a wise man."

"So how come you learned enough to be a doctor, feller?" the half-breed countered evenly, as he pushed fresh shells through the loading gate of the Winchester.

"A good memory has served me well throughout life, sir."

"Shit, Doc, let's get to this friggin' bullet wound!" Meyers snarled. "I could bleed to death!"

110

"Aye, of course," Laurie said, and his thin face abruptly showed an expression of deep-seated rancor, which also sounded in his voice. "I will remember you, sir. And if our sheriff is successful in his endeavors, I shall greatly enjoy pronouncing you dead after the noose has broken your neck."

Meyers had started across the street, unsteady on his feet as blood continued to seep from the entry- and exit-holes of the bullet wound. He came to a swaying halt and looked back to plead shakily, "Doc, for God's sake, come patch me up."

"Aye, that's a good and fine man you have made one of my patients, and—"

"Yeah," Edge cut in bleakly as he glanced at the weakening Meyers. "I hear tell that's a virtue."

CHAPTER ELEVEN

CYRUS and Amelia Benteen emerged from the office building and the lawman accepted gratefully their help to keep him from stumbling over the final few yards to Laurie's surgery, while the lanky doctor went in ahead of them to light a lamp and draw the drapes across his window.

"Don't get sick in this town, Mr. Edge," Kane Worthington said dully as he emerged from the bank. "When he's sober, that man is an excellent doctor. Drunk or sober, he does not take to hearing his medical skills decried. And there's more than one way to cure a man of what ails him."

In the bank, while his men were doing whatever was necessary to get the money they had come for, the rancher had filled and lit his pipe. And now he sucked at the stem contentedly as he raked his pale green eyes along the deserted street.

"More than one way to do most things, feller," the half-breed answered as Ralph Quine led the other men from the bank. The deputy with hatred in his eyes for Edge carried a light-weighing sack which he patted as he reported to Worthington,

"Checked it twice, sir. Exactly ten thousand to the dollar."

The rancher nodded, "Fine. Mount up, you men. We'll leave now."

Quine went to the runabout while the other deputies crossed to where their horses waited at a hitching rail outside the fire-blackened remains of what had once been a two-storey building.

"I always endeavor to do everything the right way, sir," Worthington told Edge. "But sometimes I find that my hand is forced."

"I made a comment, not a criticism, feller."

Worthington shot a sidelong look at Edge which suggested he was not quite sure whether or not to believe him. Then he cleared his throat. "This has been an ugly incident, sir. But it could have been much worse. I want to thank you. If you had not intervened, I would have killed Sheriff Meyers, you know."

"What I figured."

"You saw the kind of temper I have—when I attacked my elder daughter."

"Yeah."

"Was it she who tried to kill you? Back at the house this afternoon? It would not surprise me to hear that she tried to take revenge for the manner in which you scorned her."

"Figure that's my business, feller."

The rancher snatched the pipe from his mouth with an angry movement of his big hand. But then doused the fire of a new anger. "I heard there was shooting up on Indian Hill, Mr. Edge. After you had left to see a man named Roy Dibble. There have been rumors on the Bar-W that Dibble is one of the men May consorts with."

"Your men are waiting to leave, feller."

Worthington glanced at the mounted deputies and at his runabout with Ralph Quine in the driver's seat holding the reins. "My men are paid well to await my bidding and to do it. You'll ride with us to the Bar-W and we'll discuss the matter of my elder daughter further."

He made to swing away from Edge, but halted the action when he realized the half-breed was not going to comply.

"Two thousand dollars, sir," he reminded harshly.

"Which I ain't asking for until after you get your

younger daughter back. You bring it here tomorrow and put it in the bank. And you give me the fifty thousand to take to the Mexican. At sunup. There's nothing else to talk about."

He started across the street.

"You're crazy if you think I'll trust a man like you!" Kane Worthington snarled after him.

"Just say the word, sir!" Quine pleaded eagerly.

And when Edge halted and glanced along the street he saw that the mounted men as well as the one aboard the runabout had shifted their hands to holstered guns. Then the half-breed, uncocked Winchester still canted casually to his left shoulder, turned his head further to rake his narrowed eyes to the tense rancher in front of the bank.

"I ain't had nothing but a plate of beans in my belly all day, feller. So you want me to say it?"

Confusion over the cryptic comment drove back the rage that threatened to influence Worthington's response to Quine's request.

"Plan to eat now," Edge added. "Just say Grace."

He turned his back on Worthington, Quine and the mounted deputies and started along the street toward the corner around which he had left the gelding. And did not allow his thin lips to part in an ice-cold grin until he heard the rancher's footfalls—going away from him. Next came the clop of hooves and the creak of timber as saddle horses and the cut-under rig were turned and headed out of Indian Hill to the west.

Before this, he was aware of the dangerous possibility that he had misjudged the hard-bitten rancher with ambition for limitless power. For such a man, susceptible as he was to mindless rages, might well have been prepared—for a fatal second—to place his pride above the life or death of his younger daughter.

"You're living on borrowed time, mister. That look on his face just now, he was within a heartbeat of tellin' his gunslingers to blast you."

It was the gaunt-faced man with a beard who had

been with the other Indian Hill merchants in the saloon earlier. And he spoke as he emerged from the doorway of a darkened grocery store.

"It's been a long time since my life has been anything but a loan, feller," Edge answered evenly as he rounded the corner and whistled for the gelding.

Somewhere up on the slope north of town another horse was on the move, hooves beating at the ground in the cadence of a canter. But the moon was obscured by clouds and while the half-breed watched for a few moments, the horse never passed in front of any of the sparsely scattered squares of light that marked the windows of occupied homesteads. So he had to rely on his hearing to tell him the direction in which the horse was moving. East. He knew that an hour or so ago, May Worthington's stallion was the only horse on Indian Hill.

After he had slid the Winchester back into the boot and led the gelding out onto the broader street, he saw that the Arizona Star had become the center of attraction in town. The grocery store owner was just going between the batwing doors and the gray-faced Becker was among the dozen or so other men heading for the saloon.

Edge was aware of surreptitious ill-feeling directed toward him as he moved along the street, from the men converging on the saloon and from unseen people in the flanking buildings. The womenfolk, perhaps.

The half-breed reached the hitching rail and horse trough out front of the Arizona Star just as a middle-aged man with a clutch of warts on his jaw stepped up onto the stoop.

"Is there a livery and a place where a man can eat in this town?" Edge asked.

The man looked nervously around, as if he was afraid to be seen talking with the tall, lean stranger. "Not regular places any more," he said in a whispering tone. "But Seth Barrow will take care of your horse.

116

And Curtis Crowther who runs this saloon sometimes cooks for customers. I don't know though."

He scurried through the batwings like a frightened rabbit bolting for its hole. And, as Edge tied the reins to the rail, he heard the man announce,

"I think he's comin' inside, you men."

The words cut across and curtailed the buzz of talk which had filled the spartanly furnished and meagerly stocked saloon. Then Seth Barrow broke the silence inside as Edge's boot heel rapped on the stoop boarding.

"As owner of this place, you got the right not to serve no one you don't want to, Curtis!"

"Seems to me," the half-breed said as he halted on the threshold and slid his glinting-eyed gaze over the score or so faces turned toward him, "that nobody in this town can afford to turn away business."

"We'd rather starve than take money that's been through Kane Worthington's hands, mister!" Barrow growled. And threw what was left of a glass of whisky down his throat, then gazed ruefully into the empty glass.

"It shows," Edge drawled, shifting his narrowed eyes over the saloon again, pointedly surveying the squalor of the place and the many signs of impoverishment which the men showed in the state of their clothing and even the lines of their dejected faces. And he wrinkled his nostrils as he added, "This whole damn town stinks of defeat."

"You just helped Kane Worthington strike the final blow against us," Becker said bitterly.

"Damn right you did," the rat-faced Curtis Crowther agreed in the same tone, and received nods in response to the words. "It weren't no picnic, mister, but we was holdin' out against that bastard while he was usin' the old ways. But ain't no way we can fight hired gunslingers."

"Mr. Worthington was forced to adopt those methods," Cyrus Benteen snapped as he stepped up onto the

117

stoop and pushed past Edge to enter the saloon. "Any man worth his salt would have done the same to protect his flesh and blood."

"You're about as welcome here as the stranger, Benteen," Crowther growled. "You're as much a Worthington man as he is. Way you've been makin' money on every sale local folks was forced to make to the Bar-W."

Again there were nods and grunts of agreement from the men lounging against the bar or slumped in chairs at the tables. But a space was cleared for him at the counter and when the lawyer placed a dollar down and asked for two shots of whisky, Crowther supplied the order.

"Join me, Mr. Edge," Benteen invited with a gesture of his short arm. "And perhaps help me to make these people see sense."

"I got a horse needs taking care of, feller," the half-breed answered. "And I pay my own way."

"Shit, take care of the man's mount, Seth," the rodent-faced bartender growled. "We got enough troubles without invitin' no more."

"You take care of his friggin' horse!" the old-timer snarled.

"So keep that empty glass and keep wishin' there was liquor in it," Crowther countered wearily.

Barrow hesitated only a moment before he rose from the table and, head bent, ambled toward the door, muttering under his breath.

"Feed, water and a place to bed down is all," Edge said as the dungaree-clad old man moved around him at the doorway.

"Every man has his price," the grocery store owner said bitterly.

This after the old-timer had gone outside and raised his voice to mutter, "It won't be no pleasure, mister."

"And weaknesses," Benteen put in as Edge entered the saloon and the gap to either side of the lawyer widened.

118

The half-breed placed a dollar of his own on the bar-top before he raised the glass Benteen had left alone and took the shot of rye at a single swallow. "Like to eat," he said.

"Don't we all," Crowther answered.

Edge added a five dollar bill to the single. "Something hot, with meat. And I'll know if you've spit in it."

Crowther grimaced, moved along the bar and leaned through an archway hung with strings of beads to yell, "Blanche, bring out a plate of whatever you're cookin' for supper."

Then he returned to where Edge stood and separated the two bills, took just the single to push into a pouch at the front of his apron.

"Cover the liquor and grub both, mister. Folks in Indian Hill ain't never caught the cheatin' habit off of Kane Worthington."

"Here!" a woman shouted, and just her hand and arm were visible when she thrust a plate of steaming beef steak, grits and black eyed peas through the bead curtain.

Crowther took a knife and fork from under the bar counter and handed the food and utensils to Edge.

"Enjoy," he said grudgingly.

"Obliged," the half-breed answered and moved to an unoccupied table in a corner of the saloon.

"You sure did a turnabout over him, Curtis," the bearded owner of the grocery store complained.

Crowther spat and the saliva scored a hit into the spittoon in back of the bar counter. "Chuck made a dumb move out there against Worthington and the Bar-W guns. Took a lot of spunk, but it was dumb. Way I see it, he'd have been shot and killed for sure if this guy hadn't've winged him. And I like Chuck."

"That's right," Benteen added. "That is precisely right. Everyone who has any regard for the sheriff should be grateful to Mr. Edge."

"I'll go along with that," Becker put in.

"The sheriff didn't seem any too pleased about it," the man with warts on his jaw pointed out.

"Foolish pride," Benteen explained, and banged his glass on the bartop to call for a refill. "Sheriff Meyers had been forced by the spiteful natures of certain members of this community to take a stand in a fight he could not possibly hope to win. It is to his credit that he considered it his duty as peace officer here to take up such a position. And understandable that he resents the fact he was removed from the horns of his dilemma by the actions of an outsider."

Many pairs of eyes shifted to look at Edge as if a response was expected from him. But the half-breed appeared to be unaware of this attention, seemed not even to be listening to the talk as he finished cutting the tender steak and began to fork food into his mouth.

"Forget about Chuck standin' up to be counted when he was needed," one of the storekeepers who had been in the Arizona Star earlier growled. "I don't guess the stranger is gonna tell us why he done what he done to get the sheriff off the hook. I don't like bein' told I got a spiteful nature by no fancy-talkin' lawyer that buys his liquor with Worthington money."

There was a quality of enmity in the grunts and muttered words of agreement this time. But the short, tubby Benteen showed no sign of being frightened by the men.

"I draw my salary from the legal company for which I work," he countered. "And I can assure you gentlemen it was not my wish to uproot myself and my wife from our home in Tuscon to come down here and handle the Bar-W affairs locally. I have no bias one way or the other. Merely opinions. And I will say here and now that as a private individual I do not approve of the way Kane Worthington set out to ruin this town after he failed to gain ownership of it. But I have a job to do and I did it—ensuring that all sales and transfer were within the law."

"Nothin' legal about what that sonofabitch did at the bank," the grocery store owner growled.

"No, there wasn't, Mr. Ford," Benteen allowed regretfully. "But I can understand why he did it. Which is my point. And which you gentlemen seem determined not to acknowledge. He did not do it for the same reason that usually motivates his actions. Good God, place yourself in his position for a moment. If it was your daughter being held prisoner by those murdering Mexican bandits, would not any one of you take any desperate measure open to you in order to get her back?"

"He could've had the money without robbin' the bank," Ford answered.

"By selling you the primest land in the territory for pittance?" Benteen countered. "He's spent his entire life working toward making the Bar-W what it is today."

"Wouldn't have taken him but a few minutes of pleasure to make Grace," the man with warts on his jaw growled. "But any man worth a light would value a daughter higher than a few acres of dirt with a river runnin' across it."

This time the noisy wave of agreement that washed through the saloon did affect Cyrus Benteen. He looked exasperated and then exhausted, cast a weary-eyed gaze over the grim-faced men who showed not a trace of contrition or the slightest sign that they ever would for anything at any time.

Stretched seconds of silence elapsed, and then the half-breed at the corner table rattled his fork down on the empty plate.

"Mr. Edge." Benteen said quickly. "Don't you have anything to say?"

The half-breed got to his feet. "The lady called Blanche is a fine cook."

The lawyer squeezed his eyes tightly closed. "Please. You intervened to stem trouble out on the street. These men aren't met up in here to drown their sorrows. There must be some way to convince them not to retaliate against Worthington. That poor, unfortunate young girl who was taken by the Mexicans . . ."

"She's a Worthington, ain't she," Seth Barrow

121

growled as he re-entered the saloon. "Same as that plain-face May. Both of them as hard-nosed and high-handed as their pa. Stands to reason, them being fathered by that bastard. Why, I bet that Grace is givin' Satanas and his boys a rougher time than they're givin' her. Tough as old bootleather, them Worthington women are."

Cyrus Benteen directed a tacit plea to Edge as the half-breed made for the door and the old-timer went to the bar, hand out-stretched for the drink that had been promised him.

"I couldn't know about Grace," Edge said flatly and curled back his lips in a wry grin. "But I sure saw May's hide get tanned."

CHAPTER TWELVE

THE high cloud which had earlier veiled the moon was spread across the entire sky as the half-breed emerged from the saloon and halted briefly on the stoop to roll and light a cigarette. So there was not even the pinprick of a single star to be seen glinting against the great black dome of the heavens.

As he moved along the main and then turned onto the side street which angled north from the eastern end of the town, he sensed the same watching eyes as before. And was aware of anxiety in the minds of the watchers. But the people in the houses and the stores spared little time for Edge after they realized he was leaving town and returned their nervous attention to the front of the Arizona Star with the two wedges of yellow lamplight falling out across the stoop and half the street from the breath-misted windows and the open doorway.

There were no lights showing at the windows of the homesteads on Indian Hill as Edge climbed the trail—for the work-weary farmers and their women were all in bed—endeavoring to trade through sleep the exhaustion of the old day for a renewed store of energy to meet the next. All except Roy Dibble. He was not in his one-room house at the northern fringe of the scattering of dirt farms. And his guest of the afternoon had also left.

In the light of a flaring match, Edge closed the door which had been left open, moved to the bed and stretched out on it. He removed only his hat, and set this down on the floor instead of tipping it over his face. For the darkness beyond the window was almost as solid as that inside the room.

He reflected briefly upon the contrast between his sleeping quarters of the morning and those where he rested now. But only in the context of what a man had to be to achieve the disparate standards. Not merely to be rich or poor. Beyond this the countless problems and anxieties which the lifestyles forced upon such men—to the extent that their day-to-day lives were mapped out by the need to preserve what they had and to extend it. And in this there was little difference between Kane Worthington and Roy Dibble. Or even the other homesteaders on the hill or the people of the town at the foot of the slope.

For all of them had hopes and dreams, aims and ambitions, possessions and reputations. Which bred latent fear of losing what they had and kept them constantly hungry for that which they did not yet have.

While he lay in the dark, cold house—waiting for sleep and a caller—the man named Edge relished his own peace of mind now that he had come to accept the kind of life which his ruling fates had forced upon him.

In the distant past he had fought against such acceptance as he tried time after time to establish himself at a level somewhere between that of Roy Dibble and Kane Worthington. But events had conspired against him and eventually he had given up. But he had not smelled on himself the stink of defeat he had spoken of to the men in the Arizona Star earlier. For, in truth, it had been a victory. Because he had survived and had preserved his freedom—and came to realize that life and liberty were all he desired.

The trimmings and trappings he accepted and relished as and when they presented themselves, or just as often rejected. As he had done tonight, when he turned down the luxury of the Bar-W ranch house in favor of the Arizona Star and Roy Dibble's homestead. While he waited, not indebted to any man, to collect the two thousand dollars which would enable him to eat and to feed his horse until the money ran out.

Or perhaps he did owe somebody something. Kane Worthington the truth about the kidnapping of his younger daughter?

He vented a low, negative grunt as this doubt crossed his mind.

He had agreed to do a job and he would do it the best way he knew how. The respective probities of the various parties involved were of no concern to him. For moralizing about his fellow human beings—beyond ironic comment—was not in his nature. If people hurt him, he hurt them back. He didn't care what they did to each other.

He slept.

Then woke to the sound of footfalls approaching the homestead, the measured tread of booted feet sounding loud in the total silence of dark night as the man came across the hard-packed dirt of the yard.

Something harder than a fist banged against the door.

"Edge? You in there?" It was Chuck Meyers, his voice as grimly determined as his resolute approach to the house had been.

"Like at the Worthington place, feller. Door's open and I'm decent."

The half-breed was already up from the bed and had his hat on. He struck a match and put the flame to the wick of a ceiling-hung lamp as the door swung inwards and the Indian Hill lawman stepped across the threshold. The powerfully built man with the heavy moustache was still holding his Remington by the barrel after banging the butt against the door. He was wearing a thigh-length sheepskin coat cape-fashion over his shoulders and his right arm was held across his chest in a sling of dark-colored fabric. The skin of his round face with the high forehead was very pale. His features were set in a hard look.

125

"Where's Dibble?" he demanded.

Edge moved to the stove, rattled the grate and uttered a grunt of satisfaction when he saw red embers show through the gray ash. He pushed kindling into the stove. "I figure he was taken for a ride."

Meyers used a boot heel to crash the door closed. "It's time for some straight talkin', mister!" he snarled.

The half-breed filled a pot with water, added coffee grounds and set it on the stove. Did not respond to the lawman's angry demand until he had placed fuel on the flaming kindling. Then he straightened up, turned and nodded impassively as he moved to sit down at the table.

"What do you want to know, sheriff?" he asked evenly.

Meyers was taken by surprise at the calm response. He was still by the door and still held the Remington by the barrel. "Every damn thing," he said in a more moderate tone. And seemed to have forgotten he was holding the revolver until he waved his hand in the air. He looked at it, perplexed for a few moments, then thrust it with difficulty into a pocket of the coat. "About what happened between you and that crazy Mexican who calls himself Satanas. About what you and Worthington have cooked up together. About the shots that were fired up at this place this afternoon. About Dibble being missin'. About why you saved me from being gunned down at the bank." His narrowed eyes surveyed the sparsely furnished room while he spoke, then did a double-take at the dirt floor on the other side of the table from where Edge sat. "And about the blood that was spilled down here."

"Sure thing," the half-breed allowed as he rasped the back of a hand over the stubble on his jaw. "Always like to return a favor."

"I ain't done you any favors, mister."

"Like you to do one in the morning."

"Uh?"

"Seems like the poeple of Indian Hill are fixing to

126

make a stand against Worthington. And seems the only man they have any respect for is you. Like for you to talk them out of doing anything about what's gnawing at them until after I've got the ransom money."

Meyers listened with an expression of incredulity taking a firmer hold on his face with each word that was spoken. Then growled, "I reckon you got more gall than anyone I ever came across, mister. You don't give a shit about anyone else, do you?"

Edge did not reply to the query. Instead he gave the lawman a terse account of his run-in with the Mexican bandits, of events at the Bar-W ranch house and of what had happened with May Worthington and Roy Dibble on the farmstead.

For a while, Chuck Meyer remained incredulous as he listened to the evenly spoken words which accused Grace Worthington of being a party to her own kidnapping and her sister of trying to cash in on the treachery. But then anger rose to the surface, bringing patches of high color to the centers of his wan cheeks.

When the story was told, Edge rose to pour two cups of coffee and the sheriff sat down in the second chair at the table.

"Kane Worthington doesn't know anythin' about it not being a regular kidnappin'?" he asked as Edge resumed his seat and placed two cups of steaming coffee on the table.

"Way things turned out, it is a regular kidnapping now, feller."

"Even so . . . ?"

"From what I've seen and heard, Kane Worthington doesn't take kindly to being screwed. And if he can't have something he wants, he sets out to destroy it."

Meyers grimaced. "You ain't sayin' you're concerned for Grace?"

Edge lifted the cup in both hands and spoke over the rim after he had sipped the coffee. "If Worthington just wanted revenge, feller, he wouldn't need me."

The grimace remained in place. "And if you didn't

need me, Seth Barrow would have had another grave diggin' chore."

The half-breed said nothing. Simply looked at the lawman from out of the glinting slits of his eyes beneath their hooded lids.

"And why the hell should I do like you ask, mister? Seein' as how, if you'd leveled with Kane Worthington, there wouldn't have been no bank robbery, I wouldn't have took a bullet in the shoulder and the Worthington family's dirty linen would have been laundered a long ways from Indian Hill?"

"That's right," Edge allowed. "But what's done can't be undone, feller."

"That don't answer my question, mister. Way I see it, I can spill the whole story to Worthington. What's done can't be undone, but he'll hand back the money taken from the bank and handle things just the way he would've if you'd told him the score at the start."

The half-breed shook his head. "Not you, feller. That ain't your style. You showed that a while back when you made your stand in front of the bank. A stand against gunlaw. So you ain't going to let Worthington take the law into his own hands again, if you can help it. To go after the Mexicans who murdered those two Wells Fargo men on your patch."

"But I'll let you go?" Meyers growled sourly. "One law for you and a different one for all the rest, uh?"

Edge shrugged, an almost imperceptible rise and fall of his broad shoulders. "Like I said. Satanas told me he'll kill the woman as fast as snapping his fingers if anyone but me rides along La Hondonada at noon. You willing to find out if he's bluffing, sheriff?"

"Satanas!" Meyers rasped, and spat on the dirt floor. "He's Felipe Cortez is all. A lazy, good-for-nothin' cantina owner who most of the time was drunker than his customers!"

"Times have changed, feller. He's heading up a bunch of twenty guns now. And you ain't just got my word about how he killed those two Wells Fargo men."

The grimace expanded into a scowl and a silence lengthened in the small and squalid room that was now warmed by the stove. Then a pensive frown spread across the lawman's face and he asked, "What guarantee you got that he won't kill you, the woman and just take the money?"

"I'm being paid two thousand for my trouble," Edge replied evenly. "And I ain't got any plans to have a funeral that expensive."

"What plans do you have, mister?"

"I'll think of something."

"You gotta be kiddin'!"

Edge remained implacably silent.

"And what about May Worthington and Dibble? You reckon they rode out to Cortez's camp?"

"Spinning a coin won't tell us anything for sure."

Meyers stared hard across the table at the half-breed. Then he jerked to his feet and began to pace back and forth across the confined space of the room. The expression on his face now was one of desperate thought. Eventually he halted and slammed the heel of the fist of his left hand on the table.

"Dammit, Edge, why the frig should I trust you? And why the hell should Kane Worthington trust you?"

"How about you got no other choice, feller?"

Meyers sank wearily back onto the chair and fixed a contemptuous stare upon the half-breed's face. "Because we place a higher value on human life than we do on money."

"Guess that's an opinion of common currency, feller."

CHAPTER THIRTEEN

EDGE was seated astride the well-rested and fed gray gelding on the center of Indian Hill's main street when the sun rose and shafted its first rays at his back—to cast his shadow and that of the horse long and narrow toward the rig and riders coming in off the west trail.

The half-breed was recently washed-up and shaved and he struck a match on the stock of the booted Winchester to light his first cigarette of the day.

There was no one else on the street, but most of the town's citizens were awake, waiting with mounting tension for what was about to happen.

Edge had seen just one man since Chuck Meyers left the Dibble place, promising in grim tones that he would spend the rest of the night trying to figure out a plan of his own to save Grace Worthington and bring in Felipe Cortez. This had been Seth Barrow who had been sleeping in a barn out back of a burned-down boarding house. The barn, which the old-timer had partially converted into crude living quarters, was where the gelding was bedded down. After the horse was saddled, the half-breed nudged Barrow awake with the toe of a boot to give him a dollar for his trouble. The old-timer was bleary eyed and thick-voiced with the after-effects of too much liquor as he thanked Edge for the money—grudgingly polite and perhaps a little afraid.

Now as the mounted half-breed smoked the cigarette and waited for Kane Worthington and his men to draw close, he guessed that the dungaree-clad old man would be among the watchers contributing to the tension which seemed with each passing part of a second to be on the point of crackling in the warm sunshine of early morning.

Ralph Quine brought the cut-under rig to a halt ten feet away from where Edge waited. Craven and Kahn, Tuttle and Hanson—the thin scar of the razor-cut bared on his cheek—and the four other Bar-W men who were territorial deputies reined their horses in to either side of the runabout.

Hatred, distrust, menace and nervousness showed in varying degrees on the faces of the men wearing stars as their eyes shifted constantly in the sockets—from Edge to the neglected façades of the silent buildings and back again.

Kane Worthington, a cold pipe clenched between his teeth, was as impassive as the half-breed.

"You are a good time-keeper, sir," the rancher said grimly.

"Noon is the important time today."

Worthington took the pipe from his teeth and dug a tobacco poke from the stylish suit-jacket he wore. "Give the man the money, Ralph."

There was obvious reluctance in the way Quine lifted a pair of saddlebags from between his feet and handed them to Hanson. Who took them, moved his horse forward and held them out to Edge.

"They contain exactly what the Mexican asked for," Worthington said as Edge took the saddlebags and he tamped tobacco into his pipe bowl. While Warren Hanson backed his horse to the side of the runabout. "Show him, Ralph."

Now, from the seat between himself and the rancher, Quine picked up a long, slim envelope, opened it and fanned out the stack of hundred-dollar bills it contained.

Worthington struck a match and sucked fire into his pipe. On a cloud of aromatic smoke said, "The two thousand you asked for. It will be waiting for you when you return with my daughter."

132

"It's what we agreed, feller," Edge replied as he draped the bulging saddlebags over his own.

Worthington nodded. "An agreement of the best kind, sir. Based upon mutual trust."

The half-breed turned his horse.

"Edge!" the rancher called and the tall, lean man reined in his gelding and looked back over his shoulder, saw anguish and exhaustion on the man's face as he allowed his mask of unfeeling coldness to slip. "May has left the Bar-W. It is more important to me than ever that my young daughter is returned to me."

The half-breed confined his response to the flick of a finger against the underside of his hatbrim as he turned, cracked his eyes to the narrowest of slits against the full glare of the risen sun and heeled his mount along the eastern stretch of the street. And the clop of hooves on the hard-packed, sun-baked surface was the only sound in Indian Hill, which had never looked so much like a ghost town as it did this morning.

But up on the slope to the north some chimneys emitted smoke and here and there a dirt farmer was already out in his fields to begin another long and grueling day of toiling to stay alive.

Edge looked back just once, a few yards short of where he would ride around a curve and the town would be out of sight. And he saw that Kane Worthington and his men remained exactly as he had left them and were still the only sign of life in town.

Around the curve he asked the gelding for a canter and maintained this steady pace until he reached the meeting of the trails where the Wells Fargo stage had been held up two days earlier. His mind was a blank because any train of thought he might choose to consider was loaded with too many variables. While he rode at an easy walk out of Indian Hill and onto the open trail, he had been unable to keep his mind clear.

Kane Worthington was not by nature the kind of man to sit still and wait for things to happen. Or to trust anybody he had no power over. But what would he do if he acted according to character?

Had Chuck Meyers exerted influence on the townspeople to ensure that the dawn meeting between Worthington and Edge passed without interference? If he had done so, had it been as a component part of a plan of his own devising rather than the asked-for favor for Edge?

And what of May Worthington and Roy Dibble? Had they ridden double on the black stallion to the old *Federale* post where Grace was held by Cortez and the Mexicans? If they had, how would what they told the one-time cantina owner affect Edge?

Would a man who shot down two others—three counting Ricardo—on the slimmest of pretexts even consider keeping his word about a bargain to which he had agreed so lightly?

Speculation got Edge nowhere and he had not consciously encouraged it in the first place. So he abandoned it as he rode east and then swung south—off the trail and over the same stretch of broken terrain he had covered in the wake of the Mexicans after the hold-up. By turns walking and cantering the strong gray gelding, constantly scouring the rugged country for signs that he was being watched.

Occasionally, as the sun rose higher and became more glaringly fierce, he saw clues that men and horses had come this way. But none of the sign looked fresh. Sometimes he saw a hawk overhead. Once a flock of green jays. Here and there the spoor of a small animal or the track of a snake's passing.

For the rest just the cloudless sky, rearing rocks, sandy soil and dusty vegetation. With no mark to show where he rode from Arizona into Mexico.

He halted at about hourly intervals to take a drink from one of his canteens and to allow the horse a meager amount of the tepid water. And he guessed that it was close to nine o'clock when he dismounted at the broad mouth of the canyon known as La Hondonada, used his kerchief to mop sweat from his lean face as his slitted eyes surveyed the broken rims which were etched starkly against the blue sky until heat shimmer in the distance blurred the light and dark of the skylines.

He drank and allowed his horse to drink, then rested himself and the gelding for half an hour in the hot shade under the eastern wall of the canyon.

On his approach to the mouth of La Hondonada, he had seen that it was easier and faster to get to the rim of the western wall and it was to here that he climbed. On foot after hitching the reins of the horse to a clump of mesquite. He had unsaddled the animal so that a long wait during the hottest part of the day would be more bearable. And carried a portion of his gear up the steep climb—the bulging saddlebags over one shoulder, the two canteens over the other and gripping the Winchester in one hand.

The sun beat down on his back, sweat oozed from every pore in his body and he was breathing heavily when he got to the top. But he paused only long enough to survey the terrain in every direction from the higher vantage point. Nothing moved out there, save the optical illusion of heat shimmer which billowed like fine fabric curtains moved by stray and gentle breezes.

But, as during the morning ride from Indian Hill, he did not trust the stillness and silence and he maintained his vigilance at a high level as he moved south. He progressed as fast as the terrain and his diminishing energy allowed over a distance of two miles, to the point where La Hondonada became narrow and began to twist and turn sharply at its southern end. Then his advance slowed and he cast only infrequent glances to left and right and behind him as he concentrated upon spotting any forward sentries which Satanas might have posted.

There was one, but although the dark eyes of Nino were wide and staring, they failed to see Edge as the half-breed eased around a rock outcrop on the canyon rim at a point where the ground below started to rise toward the rim of the east-west canyon in which the Mexicans had their camp. For the eyes were part of the same death mask which contorted the acne-scarred flesh of the young Mexican's face.

The boy in the ragged clothing sat with his back propped against a boulder, one of his limp hands still loosely fisted around the ancient and battered Navy Colt in his lap. His dark hair was matted with congealed blood but an area of stark white bone showed on the crown of his head where his skull had been shattered. Dried blood-droplets on the boulder behind him told that Nino had been killed where he sat.

"Appears headaches are an occupational hazard among bandits hereabouts," the half-breed said evenly. "You still around, Sheriff?"

Chuck Meyers rose from behind the sandstone boulder against which the corpse was propped. He didn't have the sheepskin coat draped over his shoulders now. Instead, the shirt he had worn when he was shot—with the right sleeve ripped away so that the doctor could treat the wound. His arm was still in the same sling. The bristles grew thick on his face, dotted with sweat beads. His left hand was fisted around the butt of his Remington.

"It was the only way for a man with just the one arm, mister," the Indian Hill lawman growled. "Short of blastin' the kid and bringin' Cortez and his whole bunch runnin'."

Edge crossed to the boulder and saw that Nino and then Meyers had chosen a perfect vantage point—to watch the narrow end of La Hondonada and with a good view of the wooded crest of the rise beyond which was the canyon with the old *Federale* post in it.

"The people in town did like you told them," the half-breed said after he had seen as much as he needed.

Meyers seemed to require a lot of his diminished reserve of energy to suck saliva into his mouth and spit it at the boulder. "I didn't expect nothin' else. They're decent folks with respect for law and order."

"Even that kind can be pushed too far."

"Everyone has their breakin' point, mister."

"Right, feller. And you're pretty close to yours, I figure."

"Close enough. And I know myself well enough to recognize the signs, mister. If I'd stayed in town I'd have tried to enforce the law. Ridin' out here seemed a little less crazy."

"You didn't come the way I did."

The lips under the bushy moustache curled back to show an embittered grin. "Only God Almighty knows everythin', Edge. And you ain't Him. I've been a lawman hereabouts for a lot of years. Know the country real well. Hunted all over it in the old days when folks had the time and inclination for sport. With some others includin' young Dibble along. Came down here the same way he and the Worthington woman did. Must cut five miles or more off the swing you made."

They had withdrawn from the boulder as they spoke and now Edge dropped to his haunches, unburdened himself of the saddlebags, canteens and rifle and began to roll a cigarette.

"You take a look at where the Mexicans are camped, feller?"

"Yeah. Got there about sunup. In time to see the kid climb up out of the canyon and come here. Watched for an hour or so, but there wasn't any sign of life. So I came to take care of him." He gestured with the Remington toward the corpse. "And to wait for you to show up."

"You figure it was his own idea to come, feller?"

A shrug which caused him to wince as the movement of his right shoulder triggered pain. "He don't seem to live with the others. Came out of some kind of cave in the canyon wall."

"Yeah, I know about the cave," Edge muttered

137

sourly and lit the cigarette. "Figure the kid was still trying to impress Cortez. Looks like he was beating his head against a brick wall."

"Don't keep rubbin' it in, mister!" Meyers snarled. "I reckon I'll have lots of bad nights recallin' that I caved in the skull of a boy no older—"

"If it helps, feller," the half-breed interrupted, "the last time I was around here the kid was begging Cortez to let him kill me."

The lawman ran his shirt sleeve across his sweat greasy forehead and glanced up at the sky where the sun was inching toward its highest point.

"What do you have in mind?" he asked.

"Make the exchange is all."

"And if you do."

Edge rasped a hand over his jaw. "My job for Worthington is finished. Then maybe I'll consider the Wells Fargo reward. You, feller?"

"What?"

"What do you have in mind?"

Meyers scowled as he leaned against the rock outcrop around which Edge had come and from where he first saw the corpse of Nino. "My first consideration is human life, mister. And there's more than just the one at stake now. Because Dibble and May Worthington are prisoners of Cortez. And I'm here to see that you don't endanger any of those three people in your eagerness to earn that two thousand. Once they're safe, I'm goin' after Cortez. Alone, or with you. And as a duly elected lawman I'm not in line to collect any reward money."

The implied question in what he said was emphasized by the quizzical look in his eyes as he fixed his gaze on the profile of the squatting half-breed.

"Seems you ain't like me, feller," Edge responded.

"I sure ain't." He spat again. "If folks need help, I don't have to be paid money to help them."

Edge shook his head. "I meant you don't like to work single-handed."

CHAPTER FOURTEEN

THERE was a silence of several minutes duration between the two men. Broken by Sheriff Chuck Meyers when he growled,

"You know somethin', mister?"

"What?" Edge answered as he ground out his cigarette in the dust.

"I don't think you got any plan in mind. I think you're gonna play it as it comes. And if it goes wrong, you won't give a shit who gets hurt. Long as you save your own skin."

The half-breed glanced momentarily up at the glaring orb of the sun and sighed as he unfolded to his full height. "Why don't you just wait and see, feller?"

He stooped to pick up a canteen, took a drink and handed it toward Meyers, who shook his head and wiped more sweat from his forehead.

"Just make sure none of the Mexicans see you, uh? Because if they do, the prisoners are dead. Cortez said for me to come alone."

Glowering anger brought patches of color to the lawman's wan cheeks. "You really have the knack of puttin' a man over a barrel, don't you mister?"

Edge dropped the canteen and picked up the Winchester and the saddlebags. "Last time I was here, Sheriff, I wasn't in any position to make the rules. Hoping to break some on this visit." He grinned. "And it wouldn't be fair for me to ask an honest and upright man of the law to help me do that."

He started toward the boulder where the stiffening corpse of the Mexican youngster leaned.

"You make one slip up, Edge, and I'm in. No matter what you say."

The half-breed dropped to his haunches again, concealed from the hill below by the boulder. He placed the saddlebags on the ground by his feet and jacked a shell into the breech of the Winchester.

"If I make a mistake, feller," he drawled, "I figure I won't be in any position to say anything." He straightened up and glanced back at the lawman. "I'll be dead and you can do whatever the hell you want."

Then he stepped around the boulder and climbed down to where the canyon wall met the rising ground, keeping a constant watch on the jagged crest of the hill beyond which was the other canyon with the Mexicans' camp in its bottom.

There was no sign of life up there. Not even smoke from a cooking fire to smudge the clear blueness of the sky above. He also checked from time to time on the area where he had left Meyers and saw that the lawman remained hidden.

He made no attempt to conceal himself and when he reached his objective—the twenty-foot-wide entrance to the narrow end of La Hondonada—he remained in full view of anybody on the ridge. And there he stood, feet apart and body held in a relaxed attitude, the saddlebags draped over his right shoulder and the Winchester canted to his left—thumb resting on the uncocked hammer. He sweated.

Meyers was right. He had no plan—beyond keeping his side of the bargain with Felipe Cortez. And surviving if the Mexican tried to double-cross him. There could be no other way to play it in view of the rules Cortez had made and the number of men in the Mexican's band.

Once Grace Worthington was safe . . . Or even if this was not to be . . .

The half-breed licked droplets of sweat off his top lip.

Then he would go after Cortez and his actions would be dictated only by his own rules. One of which insisted that no man be allowed to cross him and go unpunished.

"Hey, *gringo!* You come, uh?"

The erstwhile cantina-owner-become-a-bandit shouted the greeting and rhetorical question from hiding at the top of the rise. And Edge allowed the breath to whistle softly out between his clenched teeth and compressed lips. Better words than a bullet.

"I don't have a twin brother, feller!" he yelled back, concentrating his slit-eyed gaze on the hump of grotesquely eroded rock where he knew Cortez was hiding.

"You alone, *gringo?*"

"You see anybody else here?"

The Mexican vented his harsh laugh. "You see nobody! But I and all my men are here!"

"I didn't bring anybody else, feller!" Edge answered truthfully, but very conscious of the presence of Chuck Meyers up on the canyon rim almost directly above him on the right. "Just the money!"

"In the saddlebags, uh?"

"Right."

"You bring the saddlebags up to me, *gringo!*"

The ice-blue eyes of the half-breed moved constantly in their sockets, raking the length of the ridge and back again, seeking the tell-tale spurt of muzzle smoke that would tell him before the crack of a report that a rifle had been fired. And his muscles remained almost painfully tensed, ready to power him sideways into the cover of a niche at the base of the canyon's wall on the right. From there, the twists and turns of the narrowest stretch of La Hondonada would place solid rock between himself and the bandits. It was a long way back to where he had left the gelding but it would take the Mexicans a long time to return to their camp, get their

141

horses and ride them up the narrow pathway out of the canyon.

"You said here, not there!"

"Now I change my mind, *gringo!*"

There was a faint echo of each shouted word, but not strong enough to distort what was being said. Edge raised a hand to touch one of the saddlebags and yelled,

"This ain't change in here, feller! Fifty thousand dollars! You won't get it if you don't do like I say!"

"What?" The Mexican's thunderous tone revealed how dangerously close he was to losing his murderous temper.

"You heard!" the half-breed countered and now there was ice-cold anger in his voice. "We made a deal and I've kept my part! You send your prisoners down here and you'll get the money!"

"Prisoners? What you mean, *gringo?*"

"Figure you've got both Worthington women and Dibble, feller!"

There was a silence in the hot stillness of the noon hour. Maybe not up on the ridge. Perhaps up there, Cortez and his men rasped angry words to each other. Then,

"Okay, *gringo!* You're smart! Comes from the Mexican part of you, I guess! The ugly sister and my old *amigo* Roy Dibble, they come here in the night! They ain't smart to figure I am still as I used to be when I run cantina!" The harsh laugh. "The fools, they think they can talk me into being as I used to be!"

"How smart are you, feller?"

"Uh?"

"Send them down here!" He shrugged a shoulder and leaned to the side, so that the bulging saddlebags dropped to the ground, and raised a billow of gray dust. "You can cover all four of us until we move back into the canyon! The money'll stay where it is!"

Another short laugh. "I can kill all four of you now, *gringo!*"

Silence again, while Cortez waited for Edge to respond. And the half-breed said nothing and did not move, except for his eyes in their narrowed lids as he watched for the puff of muzzle-smoke.

"Hey, I'm talking to you!" Getting angry again. "Why should I not kill you all now?"

"Because you don't know if there is any money in the saddlebags, feller! And I'm not going to open them and show you until Dibble and the two women are down here!"

"There is money! The great Kane Worthington had to rob the bank at Indian Hill to get it! I know this!"

"He gave me the money sure enough!"

A shorter silence now, while Cortez waited for Edge to continue. Then a roar of rage as the lack of explanation planted the seeds of doubt in the Mexican's mind.

"I kill you and look for myself!"

"And if it ain't there, where else you going to look?"

A string of curses in the Mexican's native tongue. Then,

"Okay, you *gringo* bastard! I show you how smart I am!" A figure appeared at the side of the rock where Cortez was hiding. And Edge tensed to move. Then saw it was the tall Grace Worthington, her statuesque figure attired in the man's shirt and Levis. Something was said to her and she came to a rigid halt. "This one, she come down. When she is with you, you will open the bags and show the money! If it is there, I send down the others! If it is not, you will bring it! Or I will kill the others! That a deal, *gringo?*"

"Sure!"

Another instruction was given to the beautiful red-headed woman and she moved away from the rock and started down the slope. Slowly and nervously—eyes down at the ground as if afraid she might trip and fall.

"You remember to bring something for my head-aches, *gringo?*"

"I've had a few headaches of my own, feller!"

A laugh. "*Si,* the ugly sister, she told me about some of them!"

Grace Worthington covered two hundred feet of the six hundred between the crest of the slope and where Edge waited.

"No matter! When I am rich I will be able to buy the best medicines in the world, uh?"

"Sure!"

All the Mexicans were still up on the ridge. Because of the formation of the terrain, there was no way they could have spread out to flank him without being seen. This was why he had stayed up on the canyon's rim until almost noon—to make sure Cortez did not deploy any men on the flanks. Meyers' presence was immaterial in this respect for Edge could see as much as the sheriff to the front.

"Edge!" the lawman rasped in an urgent whisper.

The half-breed acknowledged he had heard by an almost imperceptible nod.

"Men comin' along the canyon behind you!"

Another slight inclination of the head. Then, shouting louder than before, "Cortez?"

"Satanas! My name is Satanas!" The Mexican's rage made his voice even louder—shortened the odds that the men in La Hondonada could hear.

"I'm going to show you the money as soon as the woman reaches me! When I do, you send down the other two right away!"

"We agreed that, *gringo!*"

Grace Worthington was halfway down the slope now.

"They heard, but they ain't stopped!" Meyers rasped. "It's Worthington and his hired guns!"

Edge shouted, "Hurry it up, lady!"

"Roy, please save Roy," she pleaded. And she brought up her head now, to show him her haggard, tear-run face.

"Move it!" he barked.

She lengthened her stride.

Sweat trickled down the half-breed's stubbled face and pasted his clothes to his body at his chest and the small of his back. The frame of the Winchester felt

144

greasy with the salt moisture where he gripped it tightly in his left hand.

The woman broke into a run to close the final few feet to him. Then skidded to a swaying halt, legs splayed and hands coming up to press to her cheeks. Her eyes were enormously wide with horror, the stare directed to something behind Edge. To his right.

"They'll kill—" she began. And hatred clouded her pale green eyes, which moved to stare at the impassive face of Edge.

"You're okay now, Miss Grace," Ralph Quine rasped.

"Hey, *gringo,* what's—"

An animalistic grunt of rage vented from the half-breed's gritted teeth. And he lunged forward, free arm curled to encircle the woman's waist as she whirled around and screamed,

"Felipe, it's a trick!"

Then she cried a shrill sound of alarm as Edge swept her bodily off the ground, half-turned and powered for the niche in the canyon wall.

A fusillade of rifle shots exploded sounding like a hundred as the reports echoed across the hillside.

Edge felt the tug and movement of hot air as bullets snagged his clothes and cracked past his flesh. Heard the impact of the lead against rock and saw the sprays of dislodged chips.

"You cheating son of a whore!" Cortez shrieked in his native language.

Grace Worthington continued to scream shrilly, the sound changing now to that of pain when Edge slammed her viciously against the rock face.

"Not my idea, lady," the half-breed rasped, and punched her on the jaw to silence her noise and drop her into a heap on the ground. "That was."

The barrage of rifle fire was kept up for perhaps fifteen seconds, forcing Edge to crouch in the niche with the unconscious woman—and Worthington's men to remain in the cover of the canyon's first turn.

145

Then, after a hard, tense, sweating silence that lasted for just a heartbeat, Chuck Meyers yelled,

"Cortez!"

"Satanas!" the Mexican screamed. "And now you double-crossing bastards find out why I have taken this new name!"

"Wait, it wasn't—"

The lawman's protest was curtailed by the sight of May Worthington and Roy Dibble, the two staggering awkwardly out from either side of the rock which hid the Mexican bandit chief. It was obvious they had been shoved into view and equally obvious that their wrists were tied at their backs. Both of them were close to exhaustion and were drained further by the effort it took to keep from falling as they came to a halt on the sloping ground. Dibble's face was bruised and spattered with congealed blood from a beating. The woman was naked and it was her thin body that had suffered from the cruel attentions of the Mexicans.

"Holy cow!" Meyers rasped as Edge peered around his rocky cover and saw the scratches, bite marks and discoloration all over the woman's body that evidenced the viciousness of the lusting assaults against her.

"You see them both!" Cortez yelled. "Roy, he is my *amigo* and he came here because of his love for the beautiful Worthington woman! I have not harmed him! The ugly sister, she tries to tell Satanas what to do! To give him orders! So I allow my men to have their way with her! But I do not soil my hands on her!"

"Figure on account that you always have a headache," Edge growled softly.

"What do you want, Cortez?" Meyers yelled.

"Satanas, you *gringo* sonofabitch! My demand is still the same! The money! If it is not delivered to me, the ugly sister dies!"

He showed his good-looking face for just a moment. To fire a single shot. Which kicked up dirt and dust a few inches away from May Worthington's bare feet.

146

Another report cracked out a split second later. Not an echo of the first. Instead, fired from the mouth of La Hondonada.

The naked woman was flinching from the effect of the first bullet impacting so close to her. Then she became rigid and fell backwards like a toppled tree—a gout of dark crimson gushing from a hole under the small mound of her left breast.

Edge snapped his head around and saw the grim and ashen-faced Kane Worthington in a crouch, a Winchester with a smoking muzzle aimed from his shoulder. Because of the canyon mouth's formation, the rancher had only to lean to the side to be out of sight of the Mexicans on the ridge.

"You never did have anything except a couple of whorish sluts to bargain with, Cortez!" Worthington shrieked. "Now you've got nothing!"

Against a stream of Spanish invective from the top of the hill, the rancher said grimly to Edge, "You did your job, mister. I left your two thousand with Cyrus Benteen back in Indian Hill."

"Obliged, feller."

"Edge watch—" Chuck Meyers yelled from the canyon rim.

But the warning came too late. Grace Worthington had recovered consciousness without a movement or a sound to signal the fact. And now, while Edge whirled away from her father, she lunged out of cover.

"Wait, Felipe!" she called shrilly as she threw herself to the ground and gathered the saddlebags to her. "Don't harm Roy! I'll bring the money to you!"

She attempted to get to her feet, stumbled, righted herself and began to run up the slope.

"Leave it, Edge!" Kane Worthington snapped. "If she prefers a penniless dirt farmer to all that I've given and offered her, I don't care a shit about her anymore."

"But you care about money, feller," the half-breed muttered as he gazed up the slope to where the woman

147

staggered and zig-zagged in her haste to buy the life of the helpless Roy Dibble.

"You figure there ain't any in them saddlebags?" Meyers asked croakily from above. Against the sound of heavy footfalls in the mouth of La Hondonada—receding as Kane Worthington and his men withdrew.

The woman ran beyond Dibble, ignoring whatever he cried out to her. And went from sight behind the rock. After which, movement could be seen up on the ridge. Dust rose, brush quivered and here and there a man was briefly visible as the Mexicans gathered to look at the contents of the saddlebags.

"Cortez, don't—" Sheriff Meyers roared.

"Satanas!" the Mexican screamed.

And went to meet his namesake. Blown into eternity by a shattering explosion that cleaved a deep chasm across the ridge. Flame and smoke leapt into the air. And debris showered upwards and rained down. Chunks of rock and clods of earth. Bodies and parts of bodies—as black as the billowing smoke.

For stretched seconds, dust and smoke veiled the scene at the top of the slope. Then, as the ears of Edge and Meyers still rang with the after-effects of the massive explosion, the scene became still and clear.

May Worthington and Roy Dibble had been blasted a hundred feet down the slope, the man as dead as the woman now. And he almost as naked as she. Around these whole corpses were scattered arms and legs and heads and hands and feet. And unrecognizable parts of human bodies. Here and there rifles and revolvers and the twisted sections of shattered guns.

"Holy Mother of God!" Meyers groaned. "The sonofabitch must've rigged dynamite to blow soon as the bags were opened."

Edge experienced an ice-cold ball of anger in his belly as he recalled Kane Worthington's comment on handing over the saddlebags—*exactly what the Mexicans asked for*. And reflected upon the many miles he had carried the booby-trapped burden. But as he spat

148

into the dust between his feet, he brought it under control. And his tone was even when he said, "By Cortez or me, he didn't give much of a damn which."

"If you'd opened the bags, he'd have figured you were crossin' him, mister," Meyers said bitterly. "And nobody crosses Kane Worthington. Not even his flesh and blood. It takes a man like you to understand a man like that, I guess. What's that?"

Edge had taken something from his pants pocket. Now he opened his hand and allowed the hank of red hair given him by Cortez to fall and scatter to the ground.

"I figure the Mexican would have kept his end of the deal, feller. Never did do much more than harm the hair of her head."

Meyers sighed. "What I can't get is why Worthington robbed the bank if he planned to handle it this way."

"Guess he changed his plans, feller. Whatever, he asked for something and he wasn't given it. So he took it."

The half-breed turned to start back along La Honodana.

"Just be sure you don't take anythin' away from Worthington except his money, mister," the Indian Hill lawman warned.

"No sweat, feller," Edge answered. "Like I told his daughter, some people are worse off living."

Now Chuck Meyers spat and the globule of saliva hissed on the sun-heated boulder at the canyon's rim. "Crazy part of this is, that mean-hearted sonofabitch Worthington could be in line for the Wells Fargo reward money."

Edge shot a final glance back over the slope with its scattering of ripped apart corpses. "Yeah, feller," he drawled. "Tough world, ain't it. All you get is to pick up the pieces."

More bestselling western adventure from Pinnacle, America's #1 series publisher. Over 5 million copies of EDGE in print!

George G. Gilman

ADAM STEELE

More bestselling western adventure from Pinnacle, America's #1 series publisher!